# FRIENDS IN HIGH PLACES
## &
## GAMES WITH CHANCE

## ANDI MARQUETTE

FAR SEEK CHRONICLES I

Mindancer Press
Bedazzled Ink Publishing Company * Fairfield, California

© 2008 Andi Marquette

All rights reserved. No part of this publication may be reproduced or transmitted in any means, electronic or mechanical, without permission in writing from the publisher.

978-1-934452-08-0 paperback

Cover art
by
Beck McCoy

Mindancer Press
a division of
Bedazzled Ink Publishing Company
Fairfield, California

# Acknowledgements

Though writing is often a solitary journey, other beings do travel the road with those of us engaged in this hare-brained pursuit. To those of you who walked the road a bit with me during this process, many thanks to you for your insights, laughter, and suggestions. You know who you are, and at the next space port, I'll buy you a round. I also want to extend a huge shout-out to Claudia, Carrie, and Casey at Bedazzled Ink, who opted to take a chance on me, Torri, Kai, and the crew of the Far Seek. And to whatever other elves and gremlins you've got stashed over there at BI, thanks to you as well.

A major monster thanks to artist Beck McCoy for the awesome cover illustration. She has this uncanny ability to put my babblings into art and I am so honored that she agreed to create this piece for the book.

Thanks to my folks and my sister for not having that intervention when I started doing this, and thanks to them and my friends and acquaintances who have been cheering me on and putting up with my crazy ideas for . . . well, for a long time. I think I might owe you more than a few rounds at a space port. I hope my never-ending gratitude will suffice for the moment.

To my muses, without whom this definitely would not be possible, many thanks for prodding me to get back to work, and thank you, the reader, for deciding to give this a whirl. Here's hoping Torri and the gang prove as entertaining to you as they have to me.

| | |
|---|---|
| GAMES WITH CHANCE | 9 |
| FRIENDS IN HIGH PLACE | 31 |

# GAMES WITH CHANCE

Torri waited as Bultor talked briefly into his link, verifying the delivery. She spoke little Salmi, but from his satisfied grunts, he approved. She scanned the crowded room, glad he always chose this bar. Dark, noisy, and situated close to the docking bays, it provided a perfect place to conduct her business.

They sat in a corner near the front door but not in its line of sight. She watched the closest patrons, automatically checking for anything out of the ordinary. And maybe something extraordinary. Every time she came to Hallifin Port, Torri hoped that she might run into a particular bit of her past. Bultor interrupted her reconnaissance and addressed her in standard Empire, perpetuating the illusion that he was just another merchant consolidating a deal.

"I am most pleased with the condition of the cargo. You have outdone yourself. My regards to your supplier." He grinned, reptilian lips pulling back from myriad pointed teeth.

She smiled with him at the joke. He knew damn well she'd lifted the jackprobes from a Coalition freighter. He removed a palm-sized credit disk from a pocket on the inside of his jerkin and ran his taloned finger over it, programming it with the amount he and Torri had contracted thirty days prior. He placed it on the luminescent tabletop.

"I have need of medical items," he said amiably in his gravel-scraped baritone. "Tirius, in Endor Quadrant. Sixty days."

Torri calculated her options. She knew the trade routes

better in Zeta Quadrant, which was a haul to Endor through Coalition territory. That would require some maneuvering, given her outlaw status in that area. "How much?"

"Five hundred thousand."

"Done." Money like that was well worth the extra effort.

He leaned back and scratched a spot on his scaled neck. "It is most fortunate that you have visited us during Amanza. Truly the best festival in this quadrant. I recommend Shimba's for a meat pie." He drained his beverage and set the tall cylindrical container on the table then maneuvered his bulk out of the booth.

Torri watched him as he pushed through the crowd toward the entrance. She picked up the disk he'd left and pressed her thumb to its indentation. A tiny light glowed green, activating one of the many accounts she used. Once she cleared this city, she'd transfer it to yet another account. She slid the disk into a pocket on the inside of her left boot. Just as she finished, a group of five Coalition soldiers entered, all wearing their implacable black helmets, faceplates down. Not here for fun, then. No officers with them. These were rank-and-file, dressed in standard Coalition black.

She surreptitiously kept an eye on them as they moved through the crowd. One approached her table. She nodded as he passed. He ignored her, perhaps assuming she was a local. Her dark complexion and darker hair helped her pass as a member of some of the Wanderer tribes on this planet. She took a drink from her glass, let the heat of the liquid sit in her mouth for a moment before she swallowed. They were in no hurry. Probably just reminding Amanza-goers who held the balls of the city leadership.

Torri regarded the service symbol lights on the tabletop, toyed with calling for companionship. It'd been a long time since she'd enjoyed a bit of physical release with anyone. She opted against it. Payments could be traced. If she required such a thing, she'd find it in the crowd outside. Or here. She scanned the upper level, which overlooked her table, a force field ensuring no one visited the lower level via any way but the stairs. One form standing with her back toward her caught Torri's attention. She studied the figure, who turned, offering a view of her profile. Pleasantly stunned, Torri pressed the service button and within seconds a hoverdroid appeared, awaiting her order.

"A bottle of Ryzin Solstice for this table. And an empty glass to that human female there—" Torri pointed at the white-shirted figure she'd noticed at the upper-level bar. She slid her ID stick into the droid's slot and it whisked away, just over the heads of the patrons. A minute later the droid delivered her bottle along with an empty glass. It left and Torri poured herself a serving before turning to observe the upper level. The droid stopped at the appropriate woman's side, a second empty glass on its tray. Torri smiled and lifted the bottle, a question on her face when the droid's target turned and looked down at her table, puzzled. Upon seeing Torri, she started, visibly shocked, then smiled wryly and shook her head in a "you have got to be kidding" motion. But she took the glass and left the bar.

Torri waited until the white-shirted woman stood at her table. "Captain," Torri greeted her. "Care to join me in an aperitif?" She motioned toward the bottle, hoping her voice didn't betray the turbulence within.

"I'm not on duty," she said stiffly, though a current of surprise colored her tone.

Torri raised one shoulder in a shrug. "Just recognizing your accomplishments. Have a sit-down with me, Kai. It's been a long time." *Far too long.* She gestured at the empty booth on either side of her.

With an expression that said this was clearly against her better judgment, Kai slid into the seat to Torri's left. She set her glass on the table and Torri filled it. "To old friends," Torri toasted, raising an eyebrow as a strange but welcome warmth filled her gut.

"To the past," Kai retorted softly, acknowledging the toast before taking a sip. She made an appreciative noise. "You always did have good taste in liquor."

"My many travels," she said, a metaphor for the distances between them. "How are you?" She regarded Kai over the rim of her glass, noting the new crescent-shaped scar along her right cheekbone. It added more character to Kai's face, lean and serious. She still kept her sandy hair clipped short, like she had when they trained together at the Academy on Earth.

"Promoted, as you know. How did you find out?"

"My vast network of spies." Torri offered her a smile. She'd followed Kai's career since their Academy days, though she'd never tell her that.

"I know you didn't come to Hallifin to look me up." Kai set her glass on the table. "What, then?"

"Amanza. Best festival in this quadrant."

Kai snorted her disbelief.

Torri chose to ignore it. "Why hasn't the Coalition stationed you somewhere more amenable? Is the pay that good in this shit hole of a city?" She raised an eyebrow, studying Kai's reactions to her, hoping they'd changed, hoping the four years since their last conversation had closed at least one wound between them.

"Because I seem to be very good at breaking up smuggling rings." Kai held Torri's gaze then took a swallow from her glass.

Torri ignored that, as well. "Is Hallifin so riddled with vice?" she asked innocently. "There goes my relocation plan."

Kai rolled her eyes though her expression softened. "How have you been?" She spoke in Empire, and the emphasis she used carried a hint of accusation as well as concern.

"Good." Torri swirled the liquid in her glass, allowing the past a foothold. "Busy." Torri's inflection recognized and accepted the undercurrent in Kai's question, and let her know that had circumstances been different, so too might the situation between them.

"Avoiding Coalition, most likely." Kai pushed her glass around aimlessly on the table, her eyes harboring questions, the nuances of the language inviting explanation.

Torri didn't take the bait. "I avoid anyone who threatens my livelihood," she said noncommittally, though her statement carried a barb.

Kai shook her head, maybe a little sad.

"I know we still don't agree on some things," Torri said with a sigh, battling a familiar ache in her chest. "And I won't talk about them if you won't. Catch me up with your family instead. And your life. It's been nearly six years since graduation. A lot has happened. Some of which you know." *Most of which you don't.* She flashed Kai her most disarming grin. "Truce?" She raised an eyebrow, hoping to recapture the easy comradeship they'd shared in the past, and to move beyond what had happened in the collapse of the Empire. *"Alliances can be forged even in the unlikeliest of circumstances,"* droned Instructor Hani's voice through Torri's skull, from a seminar she'd had a decade ago. *"Enemies are made, not born. And trust is not something to give. It is earned."* She locked her gaze with Kai's. *Funny, the things you remember.*

"Damn you," Kai said, but she smiled. "Agreed." She pushed her glass to Torri for a refill and relaxed into the Kai who Torri remembered from their training days, the quiet but welcoming colleague, a foil to her own prickly and often fiery demeanor. They chatted amiably and shared laughter to the bottom of the bottle and when the last was poured and their glasses empty, Kai exhaled, a sound laden with what might have been regret. It lanced through Torri's heart, leaving a hole she wished she could fill. Wished she had filled years ago, before war and uncertainty came between them.

"This has been fun. Thanks." Kai sat back, her tone warm with honesty and a hint of what might have been relief.

"Care to indulge me further?" Torri coaxed. "Something to eat? You can show me the sights of Amanza."

Kai ran her fingers along the rim of her glass, a crease in her brow. "Probably not a good idea to be seen in your company on the streets," she said, though with less conviction than Torri expected.

She nodded, taking no offense. Kai's position as a Coalition soldier prevented her from willingly consorting with known criminal elements, should someone recognize Torri as such. "Perhaps another time, then. In a system less hostile to my career." *Or yours.*

"Is there such a place?" Kai teased.

Torri grinned. "I'm sure of it. And I'll let you know." She regarded Kai for a moment. "My thanks for taking the time," she said, injecting the phrase with an extra layer of meaning she wanted Kai to hear, to interpret as she wished.

"I'm glad I did." Kai pushed her empty glass aside and for a moment, she looked like she might want to add something more. The moment passed.

"Long life to you." Torri offered the Cadet salutation and held her palm up.

"And you." Kai met Torri's palm briefly with her own. Something rippled in the air between them but Kai was already on her feet and working her way through the crowd before Torri addressed it. She sat in the din for a while, thoughts roiling, before taking her leave. Other patrons occupied the table as soon as she cleared the booth, erasing her presence as effectively as if she'd never been there at all.

Torri pushed through the crowded bar to the narrow dirt streets beyond, bumping against revelers, ignoring the vendors who pulled at her sleeve and trousers for attention. Twice Escorts propositioned her, but Torri only smiled and continued on her way, accompanied by thoughts of Kai and all matter of music couched in the heavy, earthy odor of Wallowee incense. It stung her nostrils and she fought an urge to sneeze. She turned down a foul-smelling alley, littered with trash and offal, and emerged onto the adjoining street right next to Shimba's. She got in line behind a tall, wispy Shordin wearing traditional Wanderer dress and was soon engaged in conversation with a half-drunk fighter-class mechanic behind her, who amused her with tales of his ingenuity.

Once inside at the counter, a heavyset female denizen of the city waited for her order.

"I have it on expert authority that Shimba's has the best meat pies." Torri leaned against the counter, exuding nothing more than interest in a culinary experience.

"We do."

"I'd like to try your personal favorite, though I'm sure my uncle would be pleased regardless of the choice."

The other woman offered a snaggle-toothed smile. "The bistekin, then. Half a credit."

Torri slid her ID stick into the payslot and waited for her meal, which appeared wrapped in flimsy parchment that Torri eyed dubiously as the vendor handed it to her. She accepted it and left, merging once again with the sea of festival-goers outside. Her link purred in her ear. She recognized the frequency.

"Jann," she acknowledged.

"We're fueled and ready. Cyr's itching for a brainjack and I could use a drink. Saryl's agreed to stay at dock as long as we bring her Amanza cheer." His soft tenor exuded fatigue but also humor.

"What do the comms say?"

"Nothing about us."

"Then indulge. We'll leave in the morning unless something comes up." Torri broke the line with a thought and took a bite of the pie. Bultor was right about Shimba's. She chewed slowly, savoring the explosion of spices and the tenderness of the meat as it melted in her mouth. She dodged a street performer dancing with a holograph and carefully took another bite, working the meat around in her mouth until she felt the minicomm with her tongue and reached up to wipe her lips, removing Bultor's instructions with the same motion. Leaning against a nearby wall, she reached into her left boot, scratching her leg, and deposited the tiny flat rectangle into the pocket therein next to the credit disk. She continued walking and finished the pie, the wrapper already disintegrating. Torri wiped her hands on her trousers.

Time, perhaps, to find a bit of entertainment for herself. Seeing Kai had brought up some longings that she'd managed to bury in the years since they'd graduated, and since Torri broke her Academy ties in protest of Coalition policies. Why Kai continued to buy Coalition propaganda escaped her, but even that hitch between them didn't quell the connection Torri felt for her still. And in Kai's eyes, Torri saw she'd felt it, too. She stopped at a street vendor and purchased a beverage, thinking about the first time she'd met Kai, her first day at the Academy. They couldn't have been more different. And the fates as well as the Academy Instructors charged with making bunkmate assignments paired them, for the duration of their training. *"Your bunkmate is your soulmate. You will come to know her better in some ways than you know yourself. You may not like her. You may even hate her on some levels. But you will come to trust her with your life."*

Did that still hold, in the collapse of Empire and the ascent of a new, even more corrupt power? *Can I still trust you, Kai?* Torri stared into the crowd, eyes drawn to three black-clad Coalition soldiers who passed, visors on their helmets down.

*Can I trust you?* Or did Kai's uniform dispense with history, with the bond they'd created in the years of their shared training? Did Kai still exist, beyond the gray fabric of her higher rank and her Coalition obligations?

Torri's hand clutched the bottle so hard that her body heat accelerated its decomposition and some of the liquid leaked out over her fingers. Kai was a damn fine pilot, but the Coalition kept her street-bound. The finest pilot the Academy had seen in three generations. Only one other had been better, and if Torri had to cast her lot with either of them, she'd pick Kai, no hesitation. But Kai put up with the Coalition's ineptitude and absurd assignments, probably because of the money she was able to send home. Paying tithe to Coalition colonization and familial duties, trapped in the chains of responsibility and legacy. Except the Coalition took what it wanted first and then demanded payment for its protection. Why couldn't Kai see that?

Torri grimaced and drank half the contents of the container. The liquid tasted florid. She finished it and set the empty on a vendor's counter as she passed, not wanting to carry it until it completely dissolved. She wiped her hand on her shirt and followed the sound of drumming and chanting to an impromptu dance, where she linked herself arm-in-arm with various participants, trying to escape thoughts of Kai in physical exertion.

When she finally took a break, a thin Talesian promptly offered a brainjack, already half-skitted herself. Torri declined politely and extricated her arm from the other's grip three times until the Talesian raised her voice, pleading, and clamped both hands on Torri's forearm. Torri forcibly jerked her arm away, catching the attention of two Coalition soldiers who stood on the edge of the dancing frenzy, faceplates up, revealing them as human males. Torri pretended she didn't know they were interested in her and she moved nonchalantly up the street, scanning the rough mud-hewn walls for an alley.

"You there," came the brusque command in the clipped cadence of standard Coalition. Several revelers around her stopped and turned toward them. Torri did the same, knowing she'd draw even more attention if she didn't. When the others saw the soldiers weren't interested in them, they all continued on their way.

"Yes, sirs?" Torri inquired, keeping her tone level and looking from one to the other. Young. Probably fresh out of training and stationed at the seething ass-end of this quadrant. Resentful, itching for some action. Which made them dangerous. Torri opened her link as they approached, ensuring a broadcast to Saryl. Just in case.

"ID?" The taller one held out his hand.

Torri complied and he slid it into the reader strapped to his wrist.

"Antara lo Vora," he said. "Hastor." He looked up from the image on his reader, suspicious. "That's an agro-colony. What brings you to Hallifin?"

"A cargo of torset fresh from the harvest . . ." She let her voice trail off then offered him a conspiratorial smile. "And Amanza." She recognized an understanding glimmer in the shorter one's eyes. Good. She might be able to talk her way out of this if it went further.

The taller one ran another check, probably on her ship. "How long in Hastor?" he asked, not looking at her.

"Three turns."

"Originally from?" He glanced at her.

"Baltene, Vector Quadrant."

"Not conducive to farming."

"No. My parents shifted us to Cordith, then Tauren."

The shorter one glanced around, bored, but the taller wasn't ready to end the game yet. "Tauren . . . I have kin from the San Colony." He handed her ID back.

She pretended confusion. "Sir? Isn't that on Mora?" She named Tauren's largest moon. "I'm willing to be incorrect, but—"

He opened his mouth to say something more when another voice joined the conversation.

"Antara! Did our little festival lure you from the farm?" Kai stepped between the two soldiers, who immediately jerked to attention, eyes staring straight ahead.

"That and a load of torset. How are you, Captain?"

"Well, thanks. At ease," she said to the men, who relaxed. "Did you check?" She looked at the taller man.

He nodded once.

"And does anything seem amiss?"

He shook his head.

"How long left on your shifts?"

"All night, Captain," said the shorter man. Torri heard the irritation in his tone, though he masked it with the obvious deference he held for Kai. Torri had seen flashes of Kai's leadership capabilities when they were Cadets. The intervening years had obviously nurtured them.

"We're over-staffed," Kai said. "Your shifts end in two hours. It is, after all, Amanza."

He looked at her gratefully. "Two hours, Captain," he repeated with formality. Even the taller one's demeanor changed.

"Dismissed. Good work." Kai waited until the crowd swallowed them before turning her attention back to Torri and switching to Empire. "I cross-checked docking permits," she explained apologetically. "So I know the name you're—" She broke off and offered a thin smile instead.

Torri shrugged and closed the link to Saryl. "I would expect nothing less. It's your job, after all."

Kai ran a hand through her hair, a gesture Torri remembered with affection. "I'm off-duty," she said, and

Torri saw conflicting emotions in the gray of her eyes. "Any other time . . ." Her tone held an apology.

"And there'd no doubt be a different outcome here." Torri smiled, though disappointment settled along the bottom of her heart. "I don't expect favors from you. But I appreciate this one and I won't forget it. To Amanza, then." She winked and moved back into the crowds, not wanting to push her luck. Not about this. But ten steps later she turned around, narrowly avoiding bumping into a Miridian, whose feline features creased into a snarl as Torri quickly side-stepped and craned her neck. She caught sight of Kai's shirt through the throngs. Not understanding her reasons, Torri followed her, using the crowd to her advantage.

Kai led her through the heart of Hallifin, through the great square surrounded by decaying minarets that glinted gold and copper in the setting suns, tired testaments to an era before Coalition shills infiltrated and corrupted a once-proud dynasty of Tindor rulers. Torri had been through here many times before, and each time she found it less welcoming and more indicative of subterfuge and corruption. *False gods. Like every other promise the Coalition made and broke.* How strange that politics constructed the divide between her and Kai, that something like that could diminish the connection they'd built at the Academy.

Past the city center the crowds thinned like clouds in a wind until Torri was forced to hang back even farther in the shadows of the narrow streets, though Kai never once looked behind her, something out of character. Or maybe Kai had settled into herself and her routines so much during the last few years that she'd gotten complacent. *"Once a habit is established, it can't be broken without effort."* More words from a past seminar. Kai was too good a Cadet to lapse like that. More likely, she was all too aware of Torri following her. Or perhaps the uniform had clothed Kai in carelessness, even when she wasn't wearing it. The set of Kai's shoulders and her brusque stride indicated purpose, not presence, and more disappointment made Torri hang back a little farther. Had Kai forgotten her Academy days? Had Torri somehow made Kai someone she wasn't, somehow created someone from idealized memories?

They passed through another courtyard, the celebration here decidedly tamer than near the docking bays. Groups of residents sitting at tables, laughing and chatting. A musician picked a tune from his sitarri, a gentle melody that hovered above the strings. Torri fell in with two men and a woman headed in the same direction as Kai. She watched as Kai crossed the courtyard, walked beneath the arched entranceway on the opposite side, and stopped at a wide wooden door in a multi-storied stone building not fifteen paces from Torri's group. Kai pressed her thumb to the doorpad, waited, then pushed the door open, disappearing within. Probably living quarters.

Torri detached from her temporary companions and made it to the door before it closed. She placed the toe of her boot against the doorjamb. The door came to rest on the other side of her boot and Torri made a show of pretending to press her own thumb on the doorpad, suspecting surveillance pods hung on neighboring structures. She set her shoulder against the door and pushed, hoping its magnetic field hadn't yet fully engaged. It opened only a bit more so Torri increased her efforts, maintaining a steady pressure. The door relented enough for her to slide inside but before she could get her bearings in the dim interior, a hand closed on the collar of her shirt, whirled her around, and slammed her against a wall, knocking the breath momentarily from her lungs.

"I didn't take you for a common thief." Kai's words slid between her teeth like knives.

"Good," Torri managed, regaining her breath and equilibrium. "Because I'm not." She relaxed and Kai's grip loosened. Torri brought her left forearm up, knocking Kai's hand off her shirt though she felt the fabric tear. She reached with both hands before Kai recovered and gripped the front of Kai's shirt. She jerked Kai close and kissed her, a bruising, rough joining of mouths that lasted mere seconds because Kai braced both hands on the wall behind Torri's head and pushed herself back, away from Torri's lips. Shock and uncertainty flickered across her face, visible even in the gloom of the foyer.

"What in Cyllea's name are you doing?" Kai whispered, keeping her hands on the wall.

"Do you really need me to answer that?" Torri braced her back against the wall and moved her right hand to Kai's neck. She wanted Kai's lips again, wanted to feel what she wished she'd expressed five years ago but hadn't. Torri tried again to pull Kai closer. This time she met resistance, as she had with the door, but Kai's eyes reflected something else that was clearly at odds with her actions.

"Do you remember our last training flight before we graduated?" Torri kept her hand on the back of Kai's neck while her other maintained its grip on her shirt.

Kai nodded slowly, wary. "Magellan. Vector Quadrant."

"We had to shake off four drones," Torri said in a low voice, keeping her eyes on Kai's. "We picked up those other two after Vani and Jossell retreated."

"Our portside engine took a direct hit." Kai's voice softened and the muscles of her neck relaxed beneath Torri's fingers.

"You flew us back to base with one engine and six damaged thrusters, in the middle of a firefight. And then you landed without bellying." Torri unwound her left hand from Kai's shirt, let it fall to Kai's waist, where it lingered on the webbing of her belt.

"And you shot all those drones with our last working cannon. Even the Academy Council couldn't believe we pulled it off." Kai moved closer, no longer fighting, a slight smile on her lips.

"You were the best pilot in a century of Cadets." Torri's left hand worked its way to the small of Kai's back. "I'd stake my family's holding that you still are."

Kai took a small step forward, her right leg now between Torri's thighs and everything Torri had wanted to say years before expressed itself in the exhalation that escaped her throat.

"You were an amazing shot," Kai whispered, easing forward, her hips now against Torri's. "I had hoped we got assigned to the same post after graduation." Kai's hands dropped from the wall to Torri's waist and Torri felt their heat even through her shirt. "But we weren't." "*And many other things happened, as well, that I couldn't have foreseen,*" her tone conveyed.

They shared a silence, Torri seeing in Kai's eyes the Cadets they'd been and the women they'd become. "I've missed you," Torri said simply and this time, Kai initiated the kiss, which evolved into many more, raw-edged but somehow tender, until Kai stopped, breathing hard against Torri's neck, arms wrapped around her.

Torri relaxed into her, sank into the weight of years and unspoken emotions. Long minutes later Kai finally pulled away, but she held onto Torri's hands, and her eyes asked what she had never voiced. Torri smiled assent, heart pounding, and she let Kai lead her up the marble steps to her quarters, let the boundaries between the past they'd endured and the choices they'd made blur until there was only sweat and heat and a slick merging of muscle and skin, the completion of a connection that ignited beneath their lips and hands that flared far into the night, fusing past with present and leaving them tangled and spent in new memories.

And Torri fought sleep, fought the pleasant fatigue that infused her limbs in Kai's arms, strove to remain awake and cognizant of what had happened here, what might yet happen. Whether ending or beginning, she needed the reality of Kai's skin beneath her hands, of Kai's lips and her touch and the way change might feel between them. But in Kai's embrace, Torri's body overruled her mind and succumbed to the warmth and safety she felt there and she slipped into sleep, Kai's lips on her neck.

A Hallifin dawn entered the room and expanded to fill the high, domed ceilings, coaxing Torri from a doze. She pulled Kai closer, breathing her scent, now mingled with her own, and watched over Kai's shoulder as the chronometer on the granite windowsill marked the inevitable. She dreaded what was coming, but knew, too, that this was the order of things.

Kai stirred against her. "I've missed you, too," she whispered. Her fingertips drew patterns on Torri's chest that somehow leaked through her skin to the surface layers of her heart.

Torri smiled, hope lighting the years between them and she brushed her lips against Kai's forehead, willing the chronometer to stop, willing the previous night to somehow bind them closer, if only for now. She studied Kai's eyes, not bothering to hide the regret in her own. Kai kissed it away and ran her hands the length of Torri's body, stirring the night's ashes into embers then flames until the chronometer announced the unavoidable and Kai reluctantly entered the shower while Torri dressed.

They lingered at the door, both leaving possibility unspoken, and their last kiss might have been a promise though Torri knew better than to expect it. She left first, but at the bottom of the steps she turned. Kai stood at the top of the staircase, watching her, the gray of her Coalition uniform reiterating a chasm between them but she raised her right hand in a Cadet salutation, and Torri accepted it as a bridge, however tenuous. She raised her own hand then left, before her impulses overrode her intuition, and she retraced her steps to the dock, her quick, easy strides carrying her through the bleary-eyed city, and back to the gulf that separated them.

She nodded politely at an obviously hungover dock agent, who waved her through the forceshield with only a cursory check of her ID. Two Coalition soldiers lolled against a nearby wall, talking in low tones. They barely glanced at her as she passed. Their wrinkled uniforms and the dust on their boots and equipment said more than their actions. Not part of Kai's troops, Torri thought as she passed, and a perverse sense of pride about Kai and her abilities made her smile to herself, at the incongruity of her pride for Kai but her distaste at what Kai represented. *What's next? Recruiting for the Coalition?*

Torri commed Jann as she approached the ship and the hatch opened, extending into a ramp that she ascended.

"And how was *your* night?" Saryl asked with a smirk as Torri boarded, her tall frame filling the cramped entryway.

"One I won't soon forget," she responded with a grin. "I think I rather like Amanza."

Saryl raised her eyebrows. "Glad to hear it. It's about time you had a little fun."

*It was much more than that.* Torri shrugged. "Are we ready to go?"

"Of course. That's why you hired me." Saryl moved so Torri could get around her in the narrow corridor to the bridge.

"Oh, is *that* it? I thought it was your charming personality."

"There's always that." She followed Torri to the bridge.

Jann turned his red-rimmed eyes to Torri as she entered. "And did Amanza treat you well?" His throat sounded as if it had treated *him* well. As it had Cyr, who kept his head down.

"Very. We might make this festival a habit," Torri said as she slid into the right-hand seat at the control panel, punching in coordinates for Zeta Quadrant before she opened a link to docking authorities and switched into Coalition. "Cargo Vessel *Far Seek* requesting departure clearance."

"Declaration?" came the response in a guttural monotone.

"Off-loaded one full shipment of torset from Hastor."

"One moment. Checking voucher."

Torri made an adjustment on the control panel, waiting for the authorities to compare arrival and departure weights of her ship. She glanced at Jann, concentrating as he made appropriate calibrations for lift-off.

"Voucher received, Antara lo Vora. Cleared for departure in sixty seconds. Out."

Torri broke the link, and Jann's fingers flew over the controls from his station. She clicked her seat harness into place around her torso and glanced at the controls, checking readings on her crew. Everybody was strapped in and ready to go.

"Fifteen seconds," Jann intoned as Torri felt the ship's thrusters engage, a subtle shift in the power currents through the walls of the vessel. "And five . . . four . . . three . . . two . . . and lift-off." The ship jerked slightly as the magnetic docklock released. Torri took the controls and guided them to proper altitude above the bays before she accelerated. Fifteen minutes later they orbited Hallifin and Jann prepared the ship for a jump.

"I take it you've lined up more work." Saryl turned in her seat to look at Torri.

"Of course," Torri said. "Tirius needs medical supplies and I know a Coalition supplier—"

Jann snorted with amusement and Cyr groaned softly.

"You do like testing your luck," Saryl said with a laugh.

"Not luck. Options." Torri flashed her a grin then turned to watch the stars lengthen into lances of light in their hyperjump. She thought about Kai, in her Coalition uniform, preparing for another day. She knew that by now Kai had found the commdisk she'd left, might even have played it on her reader and found her message. Torri quoted it in her head. *"I hope when you're off-duty again, you might think of me."* And maybe Kai would even use it one day to contact her. Maybe.

They emerged from the jump and slowed to cruising speed. A weakness, Torri knew. That's what Kai was for her. And one day, that might prove her undoing. But oh, how she knew she'd enjoy it, no matter the outcome.

Torri reached into her boot and removed both the credit disk and Bultor's instructions. "Cyr, bring up the trade routes and find me the best ones that put us in range of Endor Quadrant with as little Coalition interference as possible. We've got thirty days."

Cyr muttered something about her synapses lacking proper impulses, and Torri smiled mischievously. "And if we're lucky, we'll find another festival."

He groaned again.

# FRIENDS IN HIGH PLACES

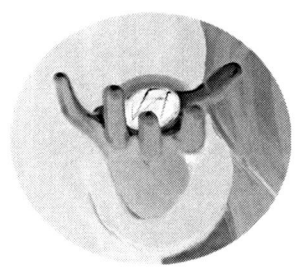

## CHAPTER 1

He was cheating. Torri read it on his face and in the way he slumped slightly to the left in his chair. She tossed a credit disk onto the pile, raising the bet and making the three other players lower their eyes to their cards. Torri studied the cheater unobtrusively, looked past his left shoulder. Ah. His partner stood, back against the bar, some twenty paces from the gamers' table. The cheater had seated himself in such a way that his back faced his accomplice. They were commlinked, then. Though the figure at the bar was only half-human, perhaps he had transmission capability, from short distances. Even standard syn parts could do that.

Torri pretended to observe the other players. She always kept her cards on a table, face-down, and the cheater's partner was staring hard at them. A soft whir sounded behind her, over her head. Server hoverdroid, no doubt part of the cheater's regimen. She listened to it engage scanning capabilities—a sharp click—and she covered her cards with her hand, a lazy movement, as if done out of long habit. Her bones and blood vessels would obstruct an accurate image.

"Show?" One of the other players grunted at the cheater, the scales on his face shifting from blue to green.

The cheater drummed the fingers of his right hand nervously on the table, studying his own cards, brow ridge lifting and falling, amber eyes narrowing.

"Bet," he growled, tossing another credit disk in. Then

from his pocket he removed an opal the size of a small egg and placed it in the center of the table. Pure-color black. Colors flared within it as light tracked over its surface. The other three players sat back on cue, as if recognizing stakes too high for their cards.

Torri glanced at the cheater's partner, who no longer leaned against the bar. Instead, he stood shifting his weight back and forth, still staring at the table, at her hand beneath which her cards remained. The droid had floated to her right, where it clicked into another scan. Torri flattened her hand against the cards, watching the cheater glance at his cards then at the droid then at his cards again. He was bluffing, but caught in some kind of bravado contest. With her free left hand, she reached for a higher denomination disk and tossed it into the pile. A few observers standing near the table muttered to each other.

"Show?" Torri raised an eyebrow and sat back, addressing the cheater in standard Empire, the language of traders and outlaws.

He grimaced and hesitated. His half-syn shill must not have offered him any insight. He looked over his cards at her, now held in both taloned hands. Torri picked up her glass in her free hand and took a sip. The liquid filled her mouth with spice and fire, ran down her throat in a smooth, hot rivulet. She set it back on the table, nonchalant. Two credit disks, both small denominations, sat within reach of the cheater's right hand. He had counted on winning this round, though Torri doubted he'd ever won an honest hand in his life.

"Show?" The player to his left nudged. From his accent, probably a native Earthman from this region. The onlookers started whispering amongst themselves, adding pressure to the cheater, who glared hard at his cards, maybe trying to divine what Torri held. The other three players all stared at him. He had little choice and placed his cards face-up on the table's milky translucent surface. The Earthman shook his head, and

Torri looked at the cheater's cards. Half-sun. Good enough to beat some, had he been a skilled player. Gazes shifted to her. She'd been right about his bluff. She flipped her cards over with her right hand, spread them out with a quick flick of her wrist.

"Full ascendant," one onlooker said, appreciative.

"Well played." Torri directed her comment to the cheater, no hint of sarcasm in her tone but in the glance she threw over his left shoulder, her meaning was clear. He scowled and pushed back from the table, bumping into observers as he headed for the door. The other players tossed their cards onto the table and drained their drinks before they, too, left. Torri waited for them to go before she stood and gathered the handful of credit disks and the opal. She'd have the house override the cheater's ID, since she had a feeling that the fool and his money weren't easily parted. She placed the disks in the right-hand cargo pocket of her BDUs and reached for her glass.

"How did you know he was cheating?" said someone in lilting Empire.

Torri took a swallow before turning to the voice, a genderless tenor that belonged to a petite female Malrusian, the irises of her eyes the color of polished jade. Torri considered her answer. Then, "Sloppy. His opening bet was too high. The best players keep their cards"—she allowed a slow smile to pull the right side of her mouth up "—and their money on their own side of the table."

The Malrusian smiled back. "Jindor." She extended her left hand, palm up.

"Syl." Torri lightly pressed her own left hand against Jindor's.

"I have a table. And a bottle. Care to join me?"

Torri drained her glass and placed it on the table. The liquor heated her throat and gut, but the Malrusian heated something else. *It has been a while.* "My pleasure. Allow me to transfer proprietorship of my winnings. Where might I find you?" She quirked an eyebrow.

Jindor motioned with her chin at a table against a wall, positioned behind the seat Torri had occupied during the game. So Jindor had been watching her. She filed that observation away and nodded once before turning into the crowd and making her way to the gamblers' counter. As she suspected, her opponent had rigged his credit disks. The attendant spent nearly ten minutes unlocking the code.

While he fussed over that, Torri examined the opal. She smiled. Had it been real, it would have come from one of the mines that spawned this dusty burrow of a city. She studied it closer. Pure-color black, mimicking Vintooth Matrix stones. A good fake, and something that might come in handy during this trip. She and her crew were here to run a shipment of real pure-color blacks, but a well-wrought synthetic could be useful. She slipped it back into her pocket and watched the attendant finish with the credit disks. Once he did, Torri programmed her own thumbprint into each. The cheater would have a rude awakening on the morrow, with his account in such a state. She transferred a tip to the attendant and returned to Jindor's table, taking a seat on the cushioned bench opposite her.

"Problem with the disks, then?" Jindor said as she opened the bottle of spirits and poured a splash into two glasses.

"My opponent isn't used to losing. But when he does, he prefers to hold on to his money as long as possible." Torri picked up her glass. "To successful evenings."

Jindor raised hers as well and tapped Torri's. "No complaints thus far." They both drank the contents of their glasses in a shot. Torri then filled each halfway.

"Care for a meal?" Torri set the bottle on the table.

"I ordered." Jindor's gaze lingered on Torri's lips then descended to her chest before returning to her face.

*A very successful evening.* Torri settled back against the

cushions as a hoverdroid arrived with a tray of small plates, each bearing a small portion of food. Jindor set the plates on the table between them. She slid a credit disk into the appropriate slot on the droid's side then arranged herself on the cushions again. Torri watched her, enjoying the way Jindor's fuchsia hair spilled down her back, and the high set of her cheekbones, offering hints about her ethnic background. Something in her voice was familiar. Torri couldn't place it. Probably reminded her of someone at the Academy.

"So what brings you to Newburg, then?" Jindor motioned for Torri to start.

"Layover," Torri said, reaching for a plate of what looked like stuffed grape leaves.

"How long?"

"A few days." Time enough to make contact with her target and plan the illicit acquisition of a shipment of opals. She bit into the grape leaf and cloves and tinnet exploded on her tongue in a cacophony of flavor. Her expression must have been obvious.

"Good food here," Jindor said, laughing. "It's popular with locals, too."

"And are you one of those?"

Jindor shrugged and picked up her glass. "For now."

Torri took another bite. Secrets. Settlements like this were built on secrets and greed. She chewed, savoring. The perfect place to do business. She caught Jindor's eye and a familiar little throb settled between her thighs. The perfect place for a lot of other things, as well. She reached for another plate.

# CHAPTER 2

Torri waited for Jindor to close the door to her living quarters before she pinned her face-first against the wall, twisting her arm behind her in a smooth, fast motion. "So. What brings *you* to Newburg?"

Jindor made a surprised sound but she didn't struggle. "Not a night with you, though I can't say I wasn't hoping."

"Business first." Torri increased the pressure on Jindor's arm. "I can't fraternize with known criminal elements." She leaned close to Jindor's ear. "Coalition rules, you know."

"Slag it." Jindor groaned. "You're Coalition? I took you for trader."

Torri released her, satisfied, and Jindor turned to face her, expression wary. "My apologies. I wasn't aware of your affiliation."

Torri pushed her against the wall again, this time gently. She put a hand on either side of Jindor's head, a smile playing on her lips. "I have no affiliation tonight."

Jindor hesitated then pulled Torri against her. "Neither do I."

"Then I believe we've taken care of business. Let's move on, shall we?"

"Please."

Torri closed her eyes as Jindor's mouth found her neck, and her fingers dug into Torri's back. *Oh, yes*. It had been a long time.

Jindor's lips worked along Torri's jaw to her mouth even as she cupped Torri's crotch. "How do you feel about additions?" she said against Torri's lips, slowly massaging Torri with her hand.

Heat and moisture flooded Torri's senses. "Very well, thank you."

"Then this is definitely going to be a successful evening." She released Torri and led her through the living area to the sleeping room.

Some hours later, Torri half-woke, a deep relaxation suffusing her limbs. She snuggled in against Jindor, breathing her in, thinking how safe it felt to be here, with Kai. She snapped completely awake. Kai? Jindor stirred and Torri removed her arm from around her, thoughts of Kai intruding on further intimacy.

She eased out of bed and dressed in the dark, and though she still tingled in places from the thoroughly enjoyable romp, a tightness lingered in her chest. She left the sleeping quarters and programmed a thank you into a commdisk that she placed on the low table in Jindor's living area. She left contact info, depending on how long Jindor was in the area. After a night like that, Torri would more than welcome another. A pleasant release, of the type she rarely afforded herself.

She removed her jammer from her left-hand cargo pocket and pressed it to the keypad, easily disabling Jindor's system. Whatever Jindor's business, it didn't lend itself to the excess security measures that anti-Coalition forces employed. Or outlaws. The door slid open and Torri stepped out into the narrow street and the stifling desert heat, like a sauna even in the pre-dawn hours. Jindor's door closed behind her and she waited a few moments, getting her bearings, listening to the distant hum and throb of mining machinery, boring through stone and sand, carving access routes that took workers sometimes miles underground.

She headed north, back toward the docking bays, and something about the air, the heat, and the dark made her think of Hallifin Port, on the ass-end of Paltor Quadrant, where she always found plenty of business. Her last trip there had brought her face to face and body to body with Captain Kai Tinsdale, leader of the Coalition barracks. Their Earth Academy days as Cadets had forged a bond between them, but in the aftermath of the Empire collapse, each chose paths that could never meet. That *should* never meet. But meet they did, Torri thought, remembering the one night they'd spent in Kai's quarters, the one instance that either had dropped her guard since they'd graduated. The one night that left so much done yet so much unsaid.

A little pang bounced through Torri's heart. She buried it and moved briskly past a Coalition patrol, whose members gave her only a passing glance. They were looking for skulkers, not people moving brazenly around a darkened mining port. Dawn lightened the eastern skies and more denizens joined Torri in the streets, most heading for the mines, by the looks of the equipment they carried. A purr in her ear alerted her to an incoming comm.

"Birrit," she acknowledged, using Saryl's alias.

"I've made arrangements for a maintenance layover. Dal's logged a hyperjump glitch that needs attending to before we pick up the shipment of tools." Saryl used Jann's alias, as well.

"And I'll be checking with the supplier in just a few minutes." Torri acknowledged the euphemism Saryl used for their next cargo. "Keep me updated on the status of the maintenance. Anything else?"

"Stricter regulations and longer searches," Saryl said blandly. "I'm making sure our permits pass. We're examining the lay of the land to see what works best."

Torri considered the information. The Coalition had sent

extra troops, as they had been threatening to do. No matter. They'd work around it. "Excellent. I'll check in with you later. Feel free to indulge in local culture."

"Acknowledged. Out."

Torri ended the communication with a thought as daylight broke, bathing Newburg in sulfur-colored light. She dug her goggles out of her BDUs and slipped the strap over her head, adjusting the eyepieces. The crowds kicked up clouds of thick reddish dust that settled on clothing, skin, and hair, and that coated the rough basalt exteriors of the squat Newburg structures. A city half-underground, buried to the shoulders in a stubborn stand against the climate. She turned left, away from the docking bays, toward the mines. She'd have a look at those later, after she met with her client. She walked another quarter mile, moving with the crowds, until she stopped at a structure a hundred yards from the closest mine.

She paused at the force shield as it recorded her body stats, and her ID and countenance flashed through the holoview. The shield crackled and disappeared, granting her entrance. T'dorrin. A name with a gypsy edge and one Torri preferred to her many other aliases. She looked gypsy, Jann liked to tell her. Three hundred years ago, he said, she'd be described as "Mediterranean." *He might be right.* She removed her goggles and put them back in her pocket.

During her Academy days, Torri flew missions over what had once been Europe. In the newer Italian settlements along the northern coast of what had been Africa, she felt a kinship with the recent settlers, who broke into song and dance in the bars every night, and welcomed her as kin. Laughing, brawling, drinking. And talking slag about the growing power of the Coalition.

Torri brushed the dust from her hair and clothing before she headed down the ramp into the bowels of Austra Province. Another city existed below the surface, and Torri followed the corridor at the bottom of the ramp into a gallery filled with eateries, vendors, and all manner of services. Newburg, like any boomtown, never slept. A kaleidoscope of sounds and smells swirled around her and she relaxed in the dissonance. Good cover for all sorts of activities that might linger on the edge of legality.

She worked her way through the throngs until she found a particular food booth and she waited for the two people in front of her before stepping forward. "Hasha," she said in Empire, sliding her ID stick into the counter slot.

The vendor, a sullen Earthwoman, filled a cylindrical vessel and handed it, steaming, to her.

"I'm looking to sell some stones," Torri said as she took the beverage. "I want the best rate. I heard Majan's is the place for that." She softened the "j" of the name, almost slurring it.

The vendor appraised her. "Depends on the stones."

"Black. From Vintooth Matrix."

The vendor eyed her closer. "Who wants to sell?"

"Syl t'Dorrin, Endor Quadrant."

The vendor said nothing, instead set to pouring another cup of hasha. Torri leaned against the counter, sipping the thick, oily liquid as she watched the crowd. She caught snatches of music, a mixture of chimes and drums. A few more customers approached and purchased food and drink. Torri moved aside for them.

"Profits depend on markets," said a melodious voice in Empire to her left.

"And markets depend on products." Torri took another sip of hasha and regarded the Miridian who stood watching her. Female, Torri deduced. She wore a deep blue diaphanous robe trimmed in some kind of silver animal fur that had probably served as dinner.

The Miridian inclined her head in acknowledgement. "Sales. Good line of work."

"Steady," Torri said noncommittally before taking another drink.

The Miridian's feline features registered no emotion. "Then let's discuss it further." She turned and moved through the crowd, not bothering to see if Torri followed. Torri set her half-empty container on the counter and tailed the Miridian, maintaining a few paces between them.

They exited the gallery and walked perhaps fifty paces down a corridor before the Miridian stopped at a heavy black curtain. Two human males stood on either side. From their physiques and weaponry, Torri deduced they were security. She scanned the corridor, noting such muscle outside every entrance within her field of vision. *Where product moves.*

One of the guards held the drape aside and the Miridian entered first. Torri waited a couple of seconds then followed. The drape fell back into place behind her. She stood a moment, allowing her eyes to adjust to the dim interior. As custom dictated, she pulled her boots off and set them by the entrance.

"Please, sit." Torri's hostess motioned at several plush cushions on the floor. "Would you care for anything to drink?"

"My thanks, but no."

The Miridian inclined her head and took a seat on one of the cushions, settling gracefully in languid, controlled movements. This then, must be Majan. Torri chose one to her right and she sat, cross-legged, waiting for her hostess to begin the contracting while she surreptitiously made note of the room's features. It reminded her of a burrow. Multi-colored tapestries covered the walls and floor and glow sockets cast soft orange circles across the jumble of cushions. White and red minerals in the black walls reflected the dim light. Another dark curtain covered a narrow entrance in the back of the room. A heavy, cloying odor hung in the close air. Animal musk, mixed with the ubiquitous tinnet of Newburg.

"You come highly recommended," Majan said. "I've also taken the liberty of checking your past."

Torri folded her hands in her lap.

"I'm pleased to report that I found nothing beyond a quaint trading background. And this gives me confidence."

Torri heard a smile of sorts in Majan's voice, though her facial musculature was incapable of rendering one. She inclined her head in acknowledgement. "I would expect nothing less than a thorough examination, given your product."

"Indeed." She ran one furred, clawed digit along her sleeve. "My client has provided a timetable, as I'm certain you're aware. The date is not negotiable. Should anything . . . untoward happen, you have your instructions."

*Lose the cargo, forfeit all payment. As well as reputation.*

Majan took Torri's silence for agreement. "You've noticed, I'm sure, the patrols. Our industry is extremely profitable and this region is privy to the best opal matrices on Earth. In several quadrants. Have you seen real stones?"

"I have."

"Then you can tell the difference between those and synthetics." It was not a question.

"I can."

Majan made a trilling noise in the back of her throat and a dark-haired Earthman, also wearing a blue robe, emerged from behind the curtain in the back of the room. He carried a flat jeweler's tray that he set on the cushion between Torri and her hostess. He straightened and took a position behind Majan, to her right.

"Twenty stones," Majan purred. "Three are real. Which are they?"

Torri gestured at the tray with her left hand. "May I?"

"Please."

Torri set the tray in her lap. Black opals all, arranged in five rows of four. Beautifully shaped, each about the length of half of

Torri's index finger. She picked one up and hefted it. A smooth, small egg in her hand. Even with the soft lighting, the inner colors of the opals flashed and glowed, shifting and melding with the crystalline outer surface at every slight movement.

"Pure-color variety are a vanity stone," Torri's hostess said pleasantly. "The Newburg mines offer the richest veins for pure-color. Which is why my client approached me." She paused. "A pure-color the size and cut you're holding now brings a hundred thousand on the open market."

"I suspect triple that in other markets." Torri glanced at her hostess. "Depending on quadrant and demand."

"Sometimes more." Majan leaned back against a stack of cushions.

Torri picked up another stone. She replaced it and held the tray up, moving it slowly from side to side, watching the light play over their surfaces. She stopped and looked up. "There are fifteen synthetics. Five real. Perhaps your assistant miscounted." Torri set the tray back on the cushion and pointed at each of the five real opals. Two in the second row and one each in rows three, four, and five.

Majan trilled again and the Earthman retrieved the tray and disappeared with it into the back. "Impressive. You'll need those skills when you pick up the shipment. I have already checked every stone, but another check is always a good idea. Especially in Newburg."

"So I gather."

"I'm expecting delivery from Vintooth in four days. City officials will be paying especially close attention to cargo in five." She leaned forward. "Especially. Close. Attention." She emphasized each word and paused before continuing. "It can't be helped. The Directive was only just applied to us last week. I recommend you have your permits in order."

*No great love for the Coalition*, Torri guessed. Which made perfect sense, since the Miridian was doing business both above- and belowground. The Coalition always disrupted business, regardless of type. And in their attempts to control and monitor black markets, they merely alienated legitimate merchants, who chafed under more and more bureaucratic restrictions. "Perhaps it would ease your mind were I and my associates to collect the shipment at the source."

Majan regarded her for a long moment.

"Or perhaps en route *from* the source," Torri proposed.

"Your idea has merit." Her eyes seemed to spark like the minerals embedded in the walls. "I like it. A glass of hasha tomorrow, then. Shintal's, near the southern shipping docks. Before the afternoon shift changes."

Torri placed her palms together and touched her index fingers to her lips, acknowledging the business deal. The Miridian trilled again in a different tone and the Earthman emerged carrying another black tray. He knelt next to Torri's hostess and held the tray out. She removed one of the credit disks and ran her thumb over its surface before placing it back in its slot. The Earthman turned, holding the tray within Torri's reach. She removed the correct disk and ran her own thumb over it.

"The other half upon delivery," Majan said. "My client is aware of the price and his part in paying it." She dismissed her servant with an imperious wave of her arm. He returned to the back and Majan once again regarded Torri for a long moment, expressionless. Her nostrils flared as she sniffed the air between them and her eyes shifted color, from pale yellow to deep green. She leaned back. "I trust your stay in Newburg will allow a bit of entertainment, at least. Should you require assistance in procuring more company . . ." She let her voice trail off.

Torri imagined herself as a strip of fur, decorating the seam of a Miridian robe. Sex, money, and greed. The triumvirate in places like Newburg. She made a mental note to shower before doing business with Miridians in the future. No doubt the scent of her previous night's activities remained on her skin. "My thanks, but I must now see to the needs of my associates."

"As you will. Well contracted, Syl t'Dorrin."

"And with you." Torri stood and backed toward the main entrance. She pulled her boots on, sliding the credit disk into the interior pocket of the left as she did so. She turned, pushed the curtain aside, and exited, blinking in the brighter light of the corridor beyond. The two guards ignored her, as she did them. All in all, a profitable two days. Perhaps she'd take another turn at the gaming tables. But first, some reconnaissance. She returned to the gallery and made her way to the surface.

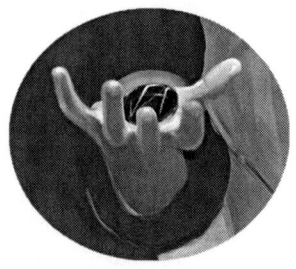

## CHAPTER 3

"What do you make of it?" Torri asked, leaning against the side of the structure closest to the mine entrance. She watched the pedestrian traffic entering and leaving, like streams of insects.

"Lax." Saryl crossed her arms. "Shitstorm of theft."

"My thoughts, too. What about at Vintooth?"

"We'll need to go have a look. From what talk I've caught, it's the matrix with the most security." She shrugged. "Makes sense, since it's where the pure-color black are."

"And it's only going to get tighter. Coalition Directive. There'll be more joining us in four days."

"They've already started," Saryl said with a wry chuckle. "Leave it to you. Never a dull moment."

"Because I know you'd be bored otherwise." Torri looked up at her. "Speaking of avoiding boredom, I know a Miridian who'd probably give you the ride of your life."

Saryl nearly choked on a laugh. "Not a trip I want to take twice."

Torri smiled. "I figured if any one of us were to engage with a Miridian, it'd be you. And you lived to tell the tale."

"Not much to tell. She'd been brainjacking. Her guard was down. Otherwise, I'd no doubt be some rug in her living quarters."

"And how would that be a bad thing? You'd make such a fine one."

Saryl snorted and Torri smiled.

"How many Coalition battalions have arrived?" Torri was more interested in the number of forces they'd have to outsmart.

"Two. Fifty each."

*Damn.*

"One dispatched to the hinterlands. No doubt Vintooth."

"And Cyr?"

Saryl didn't respond at first, and Torri read the meaning. She'd have to deal with him sooner rather than later.

"I worry about him on this exercise," Saryl finally said. "His judgment's impaired."

"Will he talk?"

"To feed the addiction, yes. He's past acceptable recreational use."

Torri nodded, acknowledging Saryl's observation but offered nothing further. Saryl would know that she'd address the matter immediately and directly. For the moment, she watched as a black-clad patrol of Coalition forces marched past and she made a disgusted noise deep in her throat. Seven years under its rule. She'd fought them actively, after she graduated from the Academy here on Earth. But the Coalition had amazing regenerative powers, establishing alliances across old enmities, throwing bones to former Empire loyalists in exchange for allegiance, no matter how superficial. Motley bands of Resistance would take out one Coalition colony, one barracks, only to see three more spring up elsewhere.

*You must pick your battles*, she remembered one of the Academy instructors droning in an art of war seminar. *And you must fight them in a way you can win. Barring that, in a way you can survive.* Lesson long since learned. *If you have but a handful of sand, use it in a way that will effectively immobilize your enemy.* Torri studied the mine's entrance. *It's not the size of the weapons, or the forces involved. It's how you employ what you have.* She had changed tactics after two Earth years. And discovered that though the Coalition weathered physical battles, proved more than willing to march an unlimited supply of warm bodies to the front lines, the High Council wasn't so willing to forfeit economic assets.

*Even the smallest insects can cause the largest beasts distress,* Instructor Derra had intoned. *Your enemies have weaknesses. Find them. Then use them.* Another group of Coalition soldiers wandered past, this one less formal than the last, their uniforms coated with Newburg dust. Some human. Others mixtures of human and syn. Still others neither. She saw how they trudged past, drained in the heat and sun, loose formation if any. Most tired. *Lax indeed.*

"What of the markets today?" Torri kept her eyes on the mines.

"Puzzling." Saryl moved closer to Torri, pushed by the movement of passersby. Her shock of hair—normally white but dyed black for this venture—jutted from her scalp like quills.

"What I don't understand is why the price of opals is so high. The production reports for the Newburg mines, at least, tell another story entirely."

Torri pushed off from the wall. "A story I want to hear. Over dinner." She led Saryl to an eatery near the offworld docks, not risking too many business discussions on board the ship. No doubt Coalition forces had already planted drones in the communication lines on board. Torri expected it, and she rarely discussed business on board her ship when docked, unless it was unavoidable. For such instances, she and her crew employed an elaborate jamming system that they could only use for a few minutes at a time, lest they alert docking officials to the nonstandard equipment on board.

Torri and Saryl entered the dark, smoky eatery and found Jann and Cyr at a table near a wall. Cyr shifted uncomfortably.

He probably wanted a brainjack. A matter of time, Torri figured, before she'd have to jettison him, as good a navigator as he was. She scrutinized him. His habit was on its way to unmanageable. The cobalt ring around his irises never faded. *Too much time within.* She made her decision then, all her instincts informing her that granting Cyr another day was like leading her crew through an unmarked minefield. They might cross unscathed. Or they might not. She was not willing to take the risk.

Torri checked Jann, pleased to see him wary but relaxed. A warrior's demeanor. He kept his scalp shaved, like the men of his home settlement generally did. Jann and Saryl she could count on. Cyr, however, might not be leaving Newburg. Torri sat in the chair to Jann's left, across from Cyr. Saryl took the remaining seat, to Torri's left.

*Loyalties are forged through either necessity or time. Sometimes both*, lectured Instructor Derra. *Loyalty derives from respect, friendship from familiarity.* Do not confuse the two. Torri studied Cyr's wiry frame across the table. He licked his lips, flicking his gaze around the room. Looking for a fellow jacker. And avoiding Torri's appraisal. She looked at Jann for confirmation. He nodded, almost imperceptibly, holding her gaze with his. *Damn.*

"Any problem getting a pass?" she asked him.

"No. Newburg is a bit less restrictive about leaving crewmembers in attendance at the docking bays. Especially if there are fewer than ten registered with a ship. Authorities were most amenable to it."

"How much did it cost?"

He grinned. "Not what you think."

She waited, amused.

"Ah, the importance of chatting up docking bay patrols. The Coordinator on duty tonight has a particular taste for Cintrello wine, something hard to come by in this province. Two bottles of that got us a pass this night."

"Well, then. I'll stop teasing you about your social proclivities," Torri said with a smile.

"I should hope so. I've saved you millions over the past few years in service fees."

Saryl started laughing.

"Okay, thousands," he amended, a little twinkle in his dark eyes.

"Must be a Volishan thing," Saryl said.

"What?" He looked at her.

"That obsession with barter." She caught Torri's eye. "Don't ever take him to a market. He haggled a merchant in Hallifin for three hours the last time we were there. Nonstop. During another festival. I left for something to eat, came back, and he was *still* working on that merchant."

"Saved us some funds." Jann shrugged good-naturedly.

"Fifty credits," Saryl pointed out, teasing him.

"Sixty," he corrected.

"Enough for one bottle of Cintrello," Torri interjected. "The darker variety."

"See?" Jann shot at Saryl. "I saved us eighty credits. A night's pass is usually two hundred."

"Which Cintrello did you give him?" Torri directed her question at Jann, but her gaze was on Cyr, who had slumped nervously in his chair, his right hand almost frenetically picking at the fabric of his shirt.

"One light, one dark."

"You saved us ninety credits, then," Torri said. "The light usually goes for fifty. Shall I promote you to Master Barterer?" she added drolly.

Jann raised his hands in a gesture of triumph. "I like it. Sort of poetic, don't you think?"

Saryl started to respond when a service droid floated over. Torri pressed the proper symbol on the tabletop so the food items displayed. They each selected a couple of dishes and Torri paid, sliding her ID stick into the droid's side. She smiled, silently thanking the cheater for his generosity at buying her *and* her crew dinner. The droid whirred away, over the heads of the crowd. Another droid appeared with a bottle of liquor and four tall glasses. Jann took the items and the droid left. Saryl poured each glass half-full. They drank a toast, though Cyr only sipped his drink. He didn't engage in the conversations about maintenance on the ship and Newburg entertainment. By the time their food arrived, his hands had started trembling, hastening Torri's decision.

"Tell me about markets," Torri said to Saryl, watching as Cyr took a couple of bites then moved his food around on his platter, scanning the crowd.

"For a pure-color black, the going rate is almost two hundred thousand. Standard size, standard cut, which is the easiest one to do. Raw pure-color black are pulling in eighty thousand. Unusual cuts—depending on the artisan and workshop—are coming in around three or four hundred thousand." She took a bite of her meat.

Torri reached for her glass. "Newburg's mines are the biggest," she mused aloud. "And the most active. What's the rate of production?"

Jann exhaled. "There's the thing. Production's at a peak right now. They're yanking enough out every day to flood the market in this quadrant and at least two others. The amount they're pulling could easily drop prices to below fifty thousand for the best-cut pure-colors. Maybe lower." He poured himself another half-glass and set the bottle on the table next to Torri. "It smells of deliberate withholding. And I'd know, being Master Barterer and all."

Torri finished her food before responding. "Sounds like something we might want to have a look at." She glanced across the table at Cyr. Sweat gleamed on his forehead and gaunt cheeks. He scratched his neck almost frantically and pain dusted his features.

Torri set her utensil down and reached into her right-hand cargo pocket for one of the disks she'd won in last night's gambling. She checked the denomination and thumbed it before setting it down in the center of the table. Saryl and Jann exchanged a glance and also set their utensils down, waiting. Cyr stopped scratching and looked at the disk then at Torri, puzzled.

"My apologies," Torri said softly. "I no longer require your services. Cyr Rollidin, you are dismissed from my crew. Take your pay." She gestured at the disk. "It includes a share for your role in this venture thus far." She used his true name, as custom dictated in such situations.

He stared at her as if she had suddenly sprouted fur.

"You can get your things tomorrow. Not before."

"You don't trust me?" He sounded plaintive, desperate.

"It has nothing to do with trust. But everything to do with performance and judgment. And both of yours, I'm afraid, are lacking."

"I haven't compromised anything," he retorted, a petulant challenge in his voice.

"Not yet. But you will."

"Think you're so fucking—"

Torri cut him off. "Since you are no longer in my employ, I cannot discipline you for insubordination." She dropped her voice, an undercurrent of warning in her tone. "But are you certain you wish to challenge me as a civilian as well?"

He looked first at Saryl, then at Jann. "So that's how it is," he said accusingly. "Use me then cut me loose in this shithole of a city."

Torri didn't respond. There was no point to arguing with him, as twisted as his thoughts had become with his addiction.

"I'm the best navigator you'll ever have," he said venomously to Torri. "Try and make your drops without me. You can't even find your way off the ship without me."

"May Cyllea guide you on your path," Torri said impassively.

Cyr leaned forward, demeanor changing. "Please," he whispered. "You need me. Who else knows the trade routes like I do? Or the ship? Please."

"My apologies," Torri said again, sadly. "I cannot take the risk. I wish you only the best. May you conquer whatever it is that drove you to this position."

Cyr's expression darkened momentarily, rage and humiliation gathering on his brow only to dissipate in seconds. He sat for a moment longer in silence then reached for the disk. He fumbled it into a trouser pocket then pushed back awkwardly from the table, the motion nearly knocking the bottle over. Saryl caught it before it spilled and Cyr stumbled into the crowd without looking back. The three sat in silence for a few minutes, adjusting to the new circumstances.

"I've made arrangements to pick up the shipment before it arrives here," Torri announced, breaking the tension. "Our Newburg client is amenable."

Jann pursed his lips and nodded in agreement as he reached for his glass, relief in his eyes and writ large across his features. "A good idea, given the patrols crawling over the mines and docking bays. I take it you have a plan?"

"Tomorrow I will. Birrit—"

Saryl grimaced. "I don't think it's a good idea to find a replacement for him here. Let's get the shipment and get away clean. We'll go to Hallifin and find another navigator. There's always someone looking for employment there."

"Not necessarily the most reputable candidates, though," Jann said. "I don't want to have to go through this again."

"Then maybe we'll find one in Vector Quadrant. We can try the military ports." Saryl reached for her glass.

Torri traced a pattern on the tabletop with her fingertip.

"Or we'll check in with Volten in Walip." Jann pushed his empty plate away. "There are always options."

Torri picked up her glass and stared meditatively into the burgundy liquid. *Yes, there are always options. It's just that sometimes, I don't like them.*

"I'll take care of the report," Saryl said, voicing Torri's thoughts. "Cyr might not be able to keep his mouth shut. Though his habit automatically makes anything he says suspect."

"He's still a risk we cannot afford to take." Torri's gaze remained on her drink. "File the report and inform the dock authorities. Play this one close to the law." *Inviting observation most often defuses it.* "He's not thinking clearly. Take extra precautions and watch your backs. The Coalition has eyes and ears everywhere. Even a jacker can get a meeting with an official if there's information to sell."

Jann nodded and drained his drink. "Good advice. In the meantime, I'll see if I can find out who might be throttling the market."

Torri relaxed. "Activate Cyr's tracker. I want to know what he does for the next couple of days. If he so much as looks at a Coalition uniform, I want to hear about it."

Saryl reached for the bottle. "I activated it when we docked, actually." She poured. "I had a bad feeling."

Torri slid her glass over to Saryl. "Were you planning on telling me this?"

She poured Torri a half-glass. "I kept hoping he'd stop."

Torri noted the unspoken "*but he didn't.*"

"And I knew that you were fully aware of his situation."

Torri pushed her own plate away. "I appreciate using your best judgment like that—"

"My apologies, Captain," Saryl interrupted, deferring to Torri's rank. "I should have told you I'd been tracking him."

Torri smiled. "I trust your judgment implicitly. We all knew about his problem. As second-in-command, you have the authority to handle the matter as you see fit unless it compromises the overall integrity of the mission and the cohesiveness of the crew. In the future, however, I'd like to know when you make a decision like that."

Jann gave her a look. "Captain Formal over here. Old habits die hard, huh?"

"If I didn't have the utmost respect for your abilities as a warrior and a beast of barter . . ." She trailed off, laughing, and took a drink. "Let's stay close to home for the next day or two. Birrit, see if you can find out how many more battalions are due as well as how many are already here. Tomorrow night we'll be able to plan our next move." She stood and the other two did as well. They exited the eatery into the night, the day's brittle heat lingering over the city. On the way back to the ship, they shared jokes and camaraderie they'd cultivated since their Resistance days, a release of sorts after what had happened with Cyr.

Torri listened as Saryl and Jann teased each other about their respective heritages. Cyr had joined them three years ago, and he had fit in, for a while. Until he lost himself to his addiction.

"Dal," Torri said, using Jann's alias. "Check for like-minds here. Maybe that's affecting the markets."

Saryl made a sound in her throat. "More likely it's Coalition."

"But the Coalition might be responding to hold-outs," Jann mused as they walked. "Good idea."

Torri thought about the client to which they were scheduled to make delivery. Not a day sooner, not a day later than what he specified. *He's anticipating a market drop.* And with the shipment, he would then corner the market. She filed that for later. They halted at the force shield that blocked the entrance to the docking bays and stood in the queue to enter. Several Coalition soldiers stood nearby, observing the pedestrian traffic. A few rested their hands on their belts while chatting with their colleagues.

Torri watched their body language, assessing. Two of the seven she'd worry about. The others were just putting in time, using Coalition forces as a ticket to something else. But the two she'd pegged as dangerous . . . fighters' edges to them. Calculating. No wasted movements. In the floodlights that surrounded the entrance to the bays, they appeared bored, the visors of their helmets up. Torri knew the look. Detached. But seeing everything. Academy trained, she felt sure. A little spark shot down her spine. Kai was a consummate soldier, a consummate leader. These two were the type Kai would recruit into a unit she commanded. *Kai*. Not the first time she'd thought of her today. And probably wouldn't be the last.

The scanner hummed, sweeping Torri's body and checking her vitals and ID. One of the soldiers Torri had pegged as Academy watched the procedure with what looked like disinterest but she knew nothing escaped him. The scan finished, Torri retracted her ID stick and stepped into the corridor as the force shield dissolved. She felt the soldier's eyes on her back as she followed Jann and Saryl down the ramp toward the maintenance hangar. They'd spend the night on the ship and tomorrow make plans to intercept the shipment from Vintooth.

## CHAPTER 4

Torri sipped her hasha, watching the mines' shipping docks, a couple hundred yards distant. Clouds of dust obscured her view but a glint of metal in the light of a swollen summer sun told her when a cargo vessel emerged from the caverns. The dust swallowed ships on slow descents to the entrances, waiting for security clearances. Floaters carrying contingents of Coalition forces whisked past at street level in all possible directions. Already, Torri felt the increased security tightening its grip, saw it in the uneasy but irritated expressions of Newburg residents or those passing through. This kind of town never welcomed regulation.

She took another drink as she stood next to the outdoor counter that squatted next to the underground entrance to Shintal's proper. This vending area served as a convenience to workers leaving the mines and those going to them and a steady flow of customers availed itself of beverages, meat pies, and maybe a couple of tokes from the hookahs set at the ends of the counter.

A familiar figure approached, and Torri concealed her surprise. Majan was thorough indeed.

"And what is your affiliation today?" Jindor said teasingly as she breached Torri's personal space and brushed her lips across Torri's mouth, an alluring gesture even though both wore goggles.

"Trader. And yours?"

"Same. In the employ of a mutual acquaintance." She smiled and rested her left hand on Torri's hip and took Torri's beverage container with her right. She indulged in a long swallow then slowly licked her lips before she handed the container back. A little ache started between Torri's thighs.

"And how long have you worked for said acquaintance?"

"Long enough," Jindor responded in such a way that answered the question Torri had implied. Majan had known when Torri and crew arrived in Newburg. Jindor's presence at the bar two nights ago was no accident.

"So it seems."

"Have you some time?" Jindor's tone conveyed two meanings.

"I might."

"I have some stones you'll be interested in. Excellent quality, already cut."

Torri let her move closer, let Jindor slide a thigh between her own, though she neither overtly welcomed nor rejected the advance.

"And some tools you might find appealing." Jindor pressed her pelvis hard against Torri's. She nipped Torri's neck and slowly pulled away. Torri knew Jindor had slipped a microcomm into her front pocket. Into Torri's right palm she placed a standard commdisk. "Should you wish to discuss this further." She swept Torri with her gaze from head to foot before turning and heading north, paralleling the mines. Torri lost sight of her in the dust and crowd.

She stood for a moment then finished the hasha just as the container dissolved. She wiped her hand on her trousers and cast a last look at the mines. Torri wanted to get inside, see how they worked. She had learned that even the most trivial bits of information might prove useful at some point. But right now, she wanted to see what Majan proposed. She smiled wryly. Majan had, indeed, done her research. Jindor was the perfect interface, encouraging not only Torri's appetites, but also the way she conducted herself. Another lesson learned, Torri thought grimly. Then again, had Majan not sent Jindor to the bar, she might not have contracted.

*Like bluffing at cards.* Don't ever show your whole hand. Not something Torri picked up in an Academy classroom, but rather something she came to understand in the disreputable bars and underground events she trolled with classmates during those years. And always, Kai at her side.

Quiet, thoughtful Kai, who easily extricated Torri from numerous scrapes, covering for her to instructors when Torri had enjoyed herself a little too much and bore the cuts, bruises, headache, and nausea to prove it. Reserved, grounded Kai, who balanced Torri's fiery spirit with a calm solidity. The kind of woman whose company Torri would never willingly have sought in her youth. But thrown together at the Academy, forced to interact, she found in Kai a companion who inspired more than friendship.

Torri spat grit onto the packed earth that served as a thoroughfare. Newburg reminded her of Hallifin in some ways, and when she thought of Hallifin, she thought of Kai. Plus, Newburg was littered with Coalition and that, too, reminded Torri of Kai. She lost herself in the stream of pedestrians and went south. She needed to check Majan's message on her wrist reader. Then she'd see what information she could gather about Vintooth. Presumably, Majan had contracted cut stones, which brought the most money. The workshops at Vintooth, thus, might be a place for gossip. Saryl was busy procuring a floater, and tonight, the two of them would take a little trip.

Torri turned west then north again, toward the mines. She stopped near an eatery with an outside counter and slid the microcomm from her pocket into her wrist reader. A constant groaning and thumping emanated from the mines at this location. Just loud enough to mask any pulse the comm might emanate but not so loud that Torri wouldn't be able to hear. She stood near a small knot of mine personnel, all laughing and talking in Empire. She played the message once, and it was crisp and clear in the link in her ear. She knew that's all Majan would have programmed into it. Sure enough, once she pulled it from the reader, the tiny stick disintegrated in her palm.

A snippet of conversation from the nearby group caught her attention. They spoke an older version of Empire, riddled with local slang, but from the discussion, Torri learned that the Coalition was curtailing shipments from outlier matrices. *Throttling the market, perhaps?* She glanced at the sky. Early afternoon threw dust storms and heat across the city's streets, which were already on their way to empty as denizens took their activities underground. Torri returned to the docking bays to see whether Saryl had managed to procure a floater. Given Majan's message, they didn't have much time. She opened a link to Saryl with a thought.

"Syl," Saryl acknowledged.

"How's the maintenance coming? Did the part come in?" Torri talked as she walked, keeping her head down against the blowing dirt.

"It did. I'm waiting to install."

"How long?"

"I have workshop access for six hours."

"I'll be there in a few minutes to help."

"Excellent. I'll file a report. Out." Saryl broke the link, and Torri quickened her pace. Six hours should be enough time. Vintooth was thirty minutes away, one way. Still, one should always plan for contingencies. She slowed down and joined the line into the hangars. Torri stood patiently, waiting to enter. The Coalition had posted double the number of guards as the night before. A reminder. Typical.

She exhaled, affecting a bored but patient air as the line moved through the checkpoint to the ID check and the force shield. Several of the guards had lowered their visors against the grit storms. They stood, faceless, either surveying the line or pulling a hapless target out for further interrogation. Torri kept her expression implacable, like the blank grey sheen of a Coalition visor.

Another Coalition floater, uncovered and loaded with twenty more soldiers, pulled up. The pilot lowered the craft a foot above the ground, and locked it into place. It bounced tightly as the newcomers disembarked in crisp military precision. Different than the group currently working the docking bay entrance. Well-trained, focused, and obviously attuned to each other. Torri watched them, her Academy past appreciating the cadence with which they left the craft and took positions in staggered recon formation, comporting themselves like well-oiled parts of a precise whole.

Only two stood between her and the force shield now. She crossed her arms and shifted her weight back and forth, presenting as a bored bystander. Another, smaller, floater arrived, this one carrying those who Torri presumed were the commanding officers of the new Coalition arrivals. The pilot lowered the vehicle, and four more Coalition soldiers off-loaded, all wearing iron grey, which indicated higher rank than the black-clothed rank-and-file. A no-nonsense contingent. And from their demeanor, all of these officers had seen field action. They didn't strut or preen, like so many officers who were granted favors and soft command posts. No, these officers had earned the maroon bars on their left biceps.

Torri located the top-ranking officer, visor also down. Female, by her body shape. The two thick maroon stripes on her arm indicated she had achieved captain, but the blue stripe underneath it broadcasted that she was on her way to promotion to commander. This assignment was no doubt part of her career path. She stood, maybe thirty paces away, back to Torri. She lifted her visor to address five of the soldiers who had arrived with the larger floater. Torri's gaze slid down the officer's back to her webbed belt. Then lower, along the lines of her ass and thighs, her breathing speeding up, partially in recognition, partially in dread. The soldier took her helmet off and shook out her short, sandy hair with an achingly familiar gesture, and Torri's breath froze in her lungs.

She tried to tear her attention away from Kai, tried to assume an air of indifference but was only partially successful. The Talesian behind her muttered under his breath at her to step lively, and she wrenched her gaze back to the force shield, automatically removing her ID stick from her shirt pocket. She slid it into the slot in the keypad and waited as her vitals flashed in the holoview.

"What's your business here?" A female guard kept her eyes on the holoview as she addressed Torri. Her two male companions stood at attention.

"Trader. Endor Quadrant."

"Expertise?"

"Stones and artisans' equipment."

The guard turned toward her. Cool, professional. Kai's contingent. "Business?"

"Orders for raw pure-colors and mid-grades. Farnessi Workshops." She kept her tone even, her expression bland. She had to get through the force shield before Kai saw her.

The guard studied the reader screen of the portable unit she held before keying the entry sequence. The force shield fizzled and the guard motioned Torri through. She brushed off in the corridor and headed down the ramp to the hangar, seeking clarity in the cadence of her boot heels on the stone floor, in the anonymity of the others sharing the space with her. An anonymity that meant nothing in the face of her past.

## CHAPTER 5

"Could be a problem," Saryl said as she studied the entrance through the magniview she held to her eyes. "There's at least one fresh battalion." She handed the magniview to Torri, who braced herself against the outcrop above the parched depression of Vintooth Matrix and adjusted the focus.

She swept the entrance and the perimeter. A landing pad sat about three hundred yards from the matrix. "Is there a back passage?"

"Not anymore. It collapsed years ago in a cave-in. Filled a mile of corridor. So the charts say."

Torri continued to assess the area through the magniview, watching how the Coalition soldiers checked everybody. A cargo craft emerged. The guards checked that, as well. "Nobody's coming or going without inspection." She lowered the magniview. "Interesting."

"Problematic." Saryl reached for the magniview and took another look.

"Majan said yesterday that the shipment leaves Vintooth in four days. I still think it's a better bet to take it en route."

"But she knows that you're planning on doing that."

Torri pursed her lips. "True. I had thought of a double-cross, as well."

"Best to be careful," Saryl said as she leaned back against the outcropping. "Especially in light of whatever's going to happen with the markets. Someone's looking to put a squeeze on."

"Coalition," Torri stated flatly. "It's got to be. Why else would they be here, cracking down on the black market? They want to control the flow of opals out of here in preparation for a squeeze." She re-tied the strip of leather that kept her hair out of her eyes. Not because it had come loose. Rather, it gave her something to do with her hands.

"Someone on the High Council?"

"Someone who's got somebody's balls in a sling. You can't just call for this many battalions if you're a local official." She exhaled. "Tell me your thoughts."

Saryl crossed her arms, her chest nearly as flat as a human man's. "The client we're making the drop to. Maybe it's him."

Torri nodded, watching dust swirl around the Vintooth entrance. "Stands to reason. I've been suspecting as much."

"Do we have a way to determine who he is?"

"You can determine anything if you name the right price. But I don't think we have that kind of time." She placed her hands on her hips, scowling. "So what we'll have to do," she said grimly, "is fuck both sides."

Saryl smiled. "And that's why I like working with you. Lots of sex."

"Speaking of which . . ." Torri threw a sidelong glance at her. "One can learn quite a lot from the right encounters."

"Such as?"

"I need a shipment of pure-color black synthetics." She took the synthetic she'd won at cards out of her pocket and handed it to her. "It'll pass. Find out who does them."

Saryl snorted. "And you think I can just walk into an eatery and find someone who can arrange that?"

"I have no doubt. Your abilities never cease to amaze me." She lightly punched Saryl on the arm. "I want a Vintooth cut and size. Fast."

"What kind of payment can we offer for these services?"

"Information." Torri turned and started hiking back up to the lip of the crater, moving carefully in the loose dirt. *Everyone has a price. It's not always money.*

Once topside, they settled themselves in the floater. Saryl had managed to secure a covered vehicle, for which Torri was eminently grateful. She buckled her harness while Saryl did the same before she disengaged the magnets and turned them back toward Newburg.

"And what kind of information are we talking about?" Saryl asked, once en route.

"Something about a potential market squeeze." Torri watched out the front window as the landscape hurtled past. "On a particular day." She settled in for the ride. "But not the day you and I suspect."

"I take it we're not going to flip the shipment en route."

"Of course we are. But not the way Majan might think."

Saryl grinned. "Another reason I like working with you. Never a dull moment." She accelerated and Torri lapsed into silence, thinking. She'd contact Jindor and see what she could extract from her. Besides, she felt the need for the kind of visit it no doubt would turn out to be.

"Have you put out a comm for a navigator?"

"This morning. An hour after I filed the report with the docking authorities."

Torri smiled. "I don't know why I bother asking."

"Your own peace of mind," Saryl responded, teasing. Then, more serious, "I expect we'll start fielding some contacts soon."

"Not to point out the obvious, but this might not be the best place for a line of potential navigators to gather outside the docking bays."

Saryl tsked. "Which is why the comm specifies digipaks only. I wanted to be sure that any suspicions about Cyr's dismissal could be deflected in a hiring process that will most likely take a while, because of my incredibly stringent requirements for the position."

"I knew there was a reason I asked you to join my crew."

"And I knew it wasn't just for my good looks."

"As much as you know that sways me," Torri said and Saryl laughed. "So can we manage this mission without Cyr?"

Saryl frowned. "The question I think you're asking is whether we can manage without a formal navigator. Cyr was a serious liability. We can definitely manage without him."

"Then the question I'm asking is what you've noted. Can we manage without a navigator?" Torri turned her head to gauge Saryl's body language. An almost imperceptible twitch occurred at the corner of Saryl's right eye.

"Yes."

"But. . ." Torri said, giving Saryl room to continue.

"It won't be easy," she admitted. "But even with Cyr, it wasn't going to be easy. And his jacking only made it that much harder. Jann and I are studying the charts. Once we get out of Earth's pull, we should be all right. Cyr did know this area, which was useful. But it's not worth our asses to have him hooked in somewhere and saying whatever fires across his neurons. The Coalition has ears everywhere." She said the last part in such a way that Torri imagined a laser slicing metal.

Torri nodded and they lapsed into silence. She lowered her goggles until they hung around her neck and rubbed her forehead. There was nothing to be done about Cyr except ensure that he wasn't spreading tales that the Coalition cared to hear. She shifted her thoughts to someone else, trying to quell her unease and strange excitement at seeing Kai again. Maybe if she could catch Kai off-duty, they could . . . Torri grimaced, dispelling the hope. Hallifin had been a fluke. But the expression in Kai's eyes that night and the next morning replayed in her mind's eye. *I'm reading too much into it.* Kai served the Coalition. Still, even in Hallifin, she hadn't turned Torri in, even knowing her past. And Torri's record made her a decent bounty for the Coalition. Why hadn't Kai turned her in? Because she honored their past as Cadets. Nothing more. Here, on Earth, with a couple more years between them, no doubt things would be different.

*War is like love*, came the words from Torri's Academy training. *You must know your adversary as your lover. Better than she knows herself. Better, perhaps, than you know even yourself.* That was the crux of effective battle strategy. Predictions based on intimacy, no matter how it was acquired. Five years she and Kai trained and lived together. By the time they graduated, they finished each other's sentences. Torri knew parts of Kai that Kai herself hadn't explored. Knew the war within her between responsibility and truth, honor and duty. Knew that what Kai showed her in Hallifin was both past and possibility. *And therein lies the problem.* Torri glared out the window. Kai knew Torri just as well.

※

"I hoped you'd want another round," Jindor said near Torri's ear. "And who are you tonight?" She braced herself on the bed, her knees between Torri's thighs, and slid her hand down Torri's abdomen.

"No one."

Jindor smiled, a mixture of sultry and secretive. The soft light from the wall's glow sockets added shadow and depth to her features, and Torri thought about the last time she'd enjoyed someone twice. Her chest tightened. *Damn.* She jerked her thoughts back to Jindor and to the expertise with which Jindor aroused her. Torri sighed in pleasure as Jindor massaged the attachment she'd affixed to Torri's crotch. It was commed into her nerves, and she felt everything Jindor did to it, everything her ministrations caused, including its stiffening. It throbbed all the way down the shaft to her clit. Jindor slipped two fingers into herself and wiped them, hot and sticky, on the attachment.

"No one seems to be very good at bringing me to certain states," Jindor said as she shifted and positioned herself over the attachment. "Not bad for a nobody."

Torri helped guide the shaft inside, exhaling sharply as Jindor's heat and moisture clamped around it. Jindor made a noise low in her throat as they moved together. Torri placed her hands on Jindor's hips, holding her in place, enjoying the way her skin felt beneath her palms, and the way the light played over Jindor's right breast and abdomen. She was careful how she placed her right hand, because the thick scar that ran from Jindor's left hip up her ribcage to the palm-sized knot of scar tissue where Jindor's left breast should have been could be sensitive. She'd learned that their first night. Jindor offered no story about the injury, and Torri didn't request one. Everybody carried scars. Some visible, some not.

Torri closed her eyes, savoring the ride, allowing sensation to build along her bones then rush over her like a thick, heavy tide but as she settled back into herself, she wished again that it was Kai who collapsed against her, panting and sweaty. She'd hold Kai all night, as she had in Hallifin, stroking her hair as Kai relaxed, arm across Torri's abdomen in a gesture both accepting and possessive. A night Torri relived many nights since then.

*My greatest weakness.* Torri stroked Jindor's back, remembering the first time she'd met Kai at the Academy barracks. How green they'd both been, Torri overbearing and cocky to hide her uncertainty, and Kai quiet and measuring, in direct contradiction. An affront, it seemed, to Torri's arrogant attitude. How disappointed Torri had been then, to discover that Kai was her bunkmate, would be her bunkmate throughout their Academy training. And for the first few months, they'd been wary, each putting up with the other because Academy rules dictated such. *Your assigned bunkmate is your closest comrade. You will eat, drink, sleep, live, and possibly die with her. You may not like her. You may come to hate the sight of her. But you will learn to trust her. With your life.*

"And who are you tomorrow?" Jindor said against Torri's shoulder.

"A prospective employer."

"Oh?" Jindor lightly ran her fingers down Torri's bare arm. "For?"

"A navigator. Mine developed a brainjacking problem, and it was interfering with his judgment." Torri put an inflection of regret in her tone.

Jindor didn't respond right away. Her fingertips tracked to Torri's thigh. "I might be able to help."

"How fortunate I am, then."

"As am I." Jindor began working the attachment again, and sparks zipped down Torri's thighs. "What sort of navigator would you like?"

"Discreet." Torri moved her pelvis in response to Jindor's touch. "Experienced, at the very least, in class two light cargo vessels . . ." she trailed off as Jindor changed her position and ran her tongue the length of the attachment.

"And?" Jindor said, before she took the length of the shaft down her throat.

"And trade routes in at least . . . six quadrants . . ." Torri groaned as Jindor released her and nipped the underside of the attachment with her teeth. Thoroughly distracted, Torri flipped Jindor onto her back with the same speed she'd employed two nights ago when she trapped her against the wall. She pinned Jindor's wrists above her head with one hand and with the other, guided her shaft inside again. *Oh, Cyllea. How good that feels.* "Perhaps a miner? Tired of a life underground?" Torri said between clenched teeth as she withdrew almost completely only to plunge in again.

Jindor gasped and strained against Torri's hips. "Harder." She hooked her heels on the backs of Torri's thighs. "Much."

Torri obliged. "Or maybe a local pilot? Wanting to expand her horizons?" She released Jindor's wrists, and Jindor grasped Torri's ass, then her back. Torri closed her eyes, wanting Kai beneath her, willing herself to feel Kai instead of Jindor. Kai's hands in her hair, lips on her mouth, heat engulfing her... Torri groaned as she released, barely stifling Kai's name.

Jindor half-howled at climax and fell back on the pillows. "I think I can help you," she said as her breathing slowed.

*Indeed you can. Though perhaps not in ways you thought.* Torri relaxed into a light doze with Jindor, waking again before dawn. As before, she slipped out of Jindor's quarters, leaving a commdisk behind. But this one was a little different. Torri made her way down the quiet streets of Newburg and activated the commdisk's tracking capabilities with her jammer. Jann was a master at jerry-rigging available technology to take on new roles.

She had no doubt that Jindor would send someone her way before early afternoon, inquiring about a navigator position. Or she'd at least supply a name. What Torri wanted to know was where Jindor went to find this someone and what role she really played in Majan's stable. Besides, there was the chance Majan might try to contact the client, especially if Jindor let slip that Torri was looking for a navigator.

Torri returned to the hangars, relieved but also disappointed that she didn't see Kai. The guards on duty obviously weren't from Kai's battalion. They let her through with barely a glance at the holoview. Torri headed to the ship, needing a shower. She also wanted to see what she might find on Kai. The commander-in-training promotion was new, within the last three months. Torri ran checks on Kai every few months, whether out of suspicion or hope she wasn't sure. Maybe both. She entered the dim hangar, waving at the guard on duty, who recognized her. He waved back. She deactivated the ship's force shield with her thumb on the nearby keypad and boarded, reactivating the shield when she did so.

This was as close to a home as she had these days. She entered her quarters, not much bigger than what she'd had at the Academy, stripped again, and availed herself of a long, hot shower, a luxury she always took advantage of when docked and hooked into a port water supply. She switched the water off and turned the drying jets on. Once done, she dressed in clean black BDUs, tan shirt, and her boots, and went to the galley to join Jann and Saryl for breakfast. They all had work to do.

## CHAPTER 6

Torri followed Jindor through the gallery, toward the commerce passageway where Torri had originally contracted with Majan. The way Jindor approached the entrance told Torri that she and the Miridian had been doing business a while. The two burly Earthmen standing guard didn't even look at Jindor as she pushed the curtain aside and slipped through. Torri studied the guards and their body language. Not much formal training. Majan had hired them for their muscle alone, and it was easy for her to remain undetected across the way, pretending to look at wares.

Saryl was on her way to a particular stone-cutter near the north entrance to the mines. Jann stayed with the ship, opting not to push their luck with port officials. Most of the time, at least one crew member had to remain with a ship in maintenance or dry-dock for the duration of a stay. There were always methods around that stipulation, and Jann had found one two days earlier. But Torri didn't want to arouse any more attention than they had in the wake of filing the termination report on Cyr.

Torri picked up a fire opal from a vendor's table, pretending to examine it. Cyr had collected his gear the day before, when Torri was waiting at Shintal's. Jann and Saryl had both been present, and both said Cyr came and went without a word. Jann wiped him from the ship's databases as soon as he had left, and Saryl said that so far, he hadn't attempted to contact the

Coalition. At least not that she could tell, which they all knew meant nothing. One didn't have to wear a uniform to be part of the Coalition network.

Torri wasn't too worried about Coalition sniffing around because of Cyr's termination, though it was best to play close to the rules for a couple of days. After all, crew came and went all the time. What worried her was Kai. She and two of her battalions were brought to Newburg specifically because Kai was good at breaking up smuggling rings. She'd said as much when they'd run across each other in Hallifin. Newburg's smuggling operations put Hallifin's to shame. And if Kai was as good as Torri suspected, that was the reason she was in Newburg.

Torri watched Majan's shop with her peripheral vision as she browsed vendors in the vicinity. Kai's skills at tracking smugglers and other brigands were near legendary in Paltor Quadrant. But then, Kai had always been good at gathering bits and pieces of information and unerringly putting them into a coherent whole. Chances were good that Kai already knew Torri was in Newburg.

Torri moved to another vendor's area, working her way through the crowds. She never worked with smuggling rings. Or even with partners. She contracted individually, which kept her out of larger networks and perhaps out of more lucrative deals, but it allowed her greater flexibility and regular clients who passed her name along to others. In addition, it provided greater safety because it was much easier for her to pass herself off as a trader, who tended to operate individually more often than not. That might give her an advantage where Kai was concerned. Kai was no doubt after the larger, more organized networks rather than the satellite outlaws. Especially if somebody in the Coalition was trying to squeeze the opal market. A few smugglers here and there—no great loss. But a large ring? Had to be shut down.

Jindor emerged from Majan's and headed back toward the gallery. Torri waited a beat then followed, keeping a distance of about thirty paces between them. Her commlink purred in her ear.

"Birrit."

"Got the tools you wanted. I've loaded them onto the ship."

"Excellent work. I'm chasing a potential sale here. I'll let you know."

"Of course. Any further instructions?"

Torri dodged a group and picked up Jindor's trail again. "Not yet. Out." She broke the link and picked up speed, keeping about twenty paces between herself and Jindor. The tracker in the commdisk would locate her easily for the next six hours, but Torri wanted to see who she interacted with. She expected the visit to Majan. Where Jindor went from there might clear up a bit of the puzzle. Torri ascended the exit ramp and pressed in with a group of miners for whom the force shield faded. She lowered her goggles as her link purred again in her ear, from the commdisk she'd left with Jindor.

"Greetings," Torri responded, moving north along the street.

"I have a name for you," Jindor said.

"And where shall I meet you, that you might impart this name?" Torri slowed her pace, still keeping Jindor in her line of vision through the crowd. Easy enough to do, given Jindor's hair color. She moved within twenty paces.

"Shintal's," Jindor announced. "Before the first evening shift."

"I'll make a point of it."

"I hope so. Nice shirt on you, by the way. Out."

Jindor broke the link and threw a glance over her left shoulder, flashing a smile at Torri before she continued on her way through the crowd. Torri slowed, letting Jindor continue.

She shook her head, grinning ruefully. So Jindor, too, was not what she seemed. Torri turned west, toward the mines, and commed Jann as she walked.

"Syl," he responded.

"What news can you give me about market prices?"

"Rates on cut stones are up and increasing. Pure-color prices are way up and shipments are tapering from the matrices. Only one, maybe two allowed a day. Morning and evening."

"I have a meeting with a potential buyer in a few hours. Any chance you and Birrit can run some figures on pure-colors?"

"Absolutely. We'll leave in thirty minutes. Out."

He broke the connection, and Torri turned north then east, toward the hangar so she could remain with the ship while Saryl and Jann determined how to pinch a shipment of pure-color black opals from Vintooth Matrix. Slag the Coalition, she thought with irritation. Something was afoot here. They'd had to bail from only one other deal in the last six years, and it was because a skirmish broke out between Coalition forces and stubborn hold-outs in Far Reach, one of the more isolated regions of Vector Quadrant.

Torri had returned the client's down payment, something almost unheard of among smugglers, but Torri liked her reputation as an honorable outlaw. The client re-hired her immediately, and they'd been doing business ever since. This, however . . . this was different. New client, recommended through one with whom she'd done business only twice. But opals guaranteed high prices on the honest market. A deal she couldn't pass up. Besides, Torri had smelled Coalition in this one. No doubt Majan's client was Coalition. Whether definite or with his nose up its ass didn't matter. He was on the take for them and for him. And Torri enjoyed fucking the Coalition whenever opportunity presented itself.

She approached the force shield to the hangars, noting the guards on duty. Not Kai's caliber. She stood in the queue, mulling the situation. She doubted she'd been set up for anything. True, the Coalition had a bounty on her, but compared to some of the larger smuggling rings, it wasn't worth the trouble. Individual hunters might profit from hauling her in, but again, there were far more expensive bounties floating around. And because she didn't work with a larger ring, she could offer no bigger prizes.

The guards pulled an Earthwoman out of the line, creating a delay in her queue. Torri maintained a placid exterior, watching as they questioned her. Nothing to be gained from it. They were just bored and trying to make their superior think they were working. She glanced at the officer, a youngish lieutenant with an unearned arrogance in the set of his chin and chest. He ignored his charges and instead turned to talk to another guard.

Torri considered the guards as they let the Earthwoman proceed into the hangars. Amateurs, like so many Coalition forces. The only thing holding this often motley group together was money. She'd met few who believed that the Coalition provided better leadership than the Empire. And the number of true Coalition loyalists she'd met she counted on one hand. Most people could be bought, she knew. And most would keep their mouths shut about their inclinations.

She stepped forward and slid her ID stick into the keypad then withdrew it. The guard waved her through without looking up from his holoreader. The force shield dissolved, and she and three others from adjoining queues entered the corridor to the hangars. A few minutes later, Torri arrived at the ship. Saryl and Jann had plenty of time to check Vintooth, do a little bit of investigation, and return before Torri had to meet Jindor later that day. She checked in with them, and ten minutes later they left, on their way to a floater rendezvous.

Once Saryl and Jann left, Torri removed the porta-case, about two feet square, from the smugglers' cache she and Jann had built into the cargo bay of the ship, camouflaged behind a ballast and hydraulic control panel. Antiquated, Saryl teased them. But the funny thing was, it worked. Torri overrode the temporary code and opened it. Ten jewelers' trays sat within. One full opal shipment. She flipped each one open and inspected all the synthetics therein, ten per tray. She held one up, watching the light play across it and fire its interior structure. A good fake. Almost as good as Majan's. Most onlookers wouldn't be able to tell the difference. And that's what Torri was counting on. She returned the synthetic to its slot and closed the tray. She rearranged the case's contents and reprogrammed it with her own code before she returned it to the cache.

Once done with that, she busied herself with a routine maintenance check of the ship's vitals, taken at four different control panels. She then ran a check on systems from the bridge, making a few pressurization adjustments and calibrating the overall system. It was something she automatically did, though Jann and Saryl handled most engineering on the ship. She logged her check and went back through Jann's notations. The main commlink on the bridge beeped, and a voice Torri knew only too well filled the bridge.

"Trader t'Dorrin, request authorization to board. Routine security check."

Torri froze and stared at the link on the control panel, at its glowing blue light and the way it triggered dread and excitement. She caught herself and turned the viewer on. Kai. In uniform and accompanied by two fellow Coalition guards.

"Authorization granted. Proceed." Torri left the bridge, feet moving automatically down the corridor to the side entrance where she entered the sequence that would open the hatch. It hissed and whirred as it did so, extending a ramp. Torri stood waiting, hands on her hips, staring down at Kai, who watched her from the hangar tarmac ten feet below.

The ramp settled but Kai hesitated, and Torri read

uncertainty in her gaze, in the grey of her eyes, and the way her brow furrowed for a few seconds. Kai's expression hardened then into her customary professional veneer, and she boarded, followed by the two male guards, coming to stand barely an arm's length from Torri.

"Captain," Torri said conversationally, hoping Kai wouldn't hear the tremor that bounced around her throat or the way her heart echoed through her torso. "Welcome aboard." She acknowledged the other two with a nod in their direction. They maintained silence.

"My apologies, Trader," Kai said crisply. "Current Directives require a full security check every two days."

Torri offered a half-smile. "Of course. I presume that involves the log and a scan?"

Kai's right shoulder shifted. A movement so slight that it might not have registered with anyone who hadn't spent years around her. The gesture told Torri that Kai had relaxed, though she maintained a cool wariness. "Please."

Torri led them to the bridge. One of the guards stood as tall as Saryl, and he had to duck his head in the cramped corridor. Torri's fingers danced over the glowing symbols on the dashboard as she overrode the security system. She then stood aside while the shorter guard held his reader over the instrument panel, jacking into the system.

"If I may ask," Kai said, watching her underling run his scan while the other stood stone-faced next to him. "Your business here?"

Torri recognized the question for what it was. An out. An unspoken chance for her to dispel any suspicions about what she was about here in another city riddled with crime. "A shipment of tools for the Farnessi Workshops in Endor Quadrant. My crew is currently making arrangements."

"Have you set a departure date?" Kai turned to her again. Her face betrayed no recognition but Torri saw in her eyes something that might have been interest in discussions beyond the professional. Or it might just have been Torri's overactive imagination.

"We were hoping to leave in two days, but one of our suppliers is having some trouble finding the correct lasers for a particular type of gem-cutter. Are you familiar with stonework, Captain?" Torri arched an eyebrow just a bit.

"Somewhat."

"Then I'm sure you'll understand how choosy artisans can be. Farnessi requires a laser calibrated for a specific silica content in pure-color opals from two separate matrices in this province. We've procured one but not the other." She shrugged. "Our supplier assures us the others will be ready either tomorrow or the next day. So we wait." She offered a "what can you do?" smile. "Shall I file a declaration of intent with docking authorities?"

"Clear, Captain," interrupted the guard running the scan.

Torri kept her gaze on Kai's eyes and saw what might have been relief in them.

"No, no need for that," Kai responded to Torri's original question. She paused before carefully launching into her next question. "You filed a termination report on Rozin Hester," she continued, more for the benefit of her accompaniment than for her own edification. Keeping up appearances. Torri knew that Kai was aware Rozin was one of Cyr's aliases. Again, a way for Torri to explain herself, skirting the boundaries of legality.

"My second-in-command did. I regret to say that Rozin was spending too much time with a pursuit that hindered his ability to serve effectively. I'm sure you understand the damage certain habits can do to a unit's cohesiveness."

Kai's right shoulder relaxed again, in the subtle motion that Torri was certain Kai didn't know she employed. "Regretful."

"It was. And another reason we've had to stay an extra day

or two. I was hoping to hire a temporary replacement." Torri sighed.

"Good luck."

"My thanks. It's needed."

Kai inclined her head. "May we check your cargo bay?"

"Please." Torri led them from the bridge to the bay, where she had so recently secured the case of synthetic opals. The guard who ran the check on the bridge did so here, as well, standing with his fellow guard at the control panel, looking at the readings. Kai stood watching them, hands resting on her belt. Torri positioned herself at the entrance into the bay, affording herself a view of Kai's profile from the right side. The crescent-shaped scar on Kai's cheekbone hadn't faded since Torri first noticed it in Hallifin. Maybe a few more lines at the corner of Kai's eyes. The same strong, lean features that she'd had since graduation. And when she let her jaw relax, so too did her mouth and in those instances, her lips were invitations that Torri had finally answered in full two years ago, five years after graduation. Her gaze remained on Kai's lips. *Cyllea, I'd do it again, given the chance. Without a second thought.*

Kai turned suddenly, catching Torri regarding her. The set of Kai's jaw sent a warning but the glint in her eyes offered something else.

"Clear, Captain," the guard said. He walked the reader to her for official validation. Kai checked the screen then pressed her thumb to it. She handed it back to her underling and looked again at Torri.

"Many thanks for your patience," she said, and Torri read things into the statement she knew were matters for dreams. But she liked the sparks that zigzagged around her ribcage at the thoughts.

"Of course." She led them back to the side entrance, lingering at the top of the ramp, watching as the two guards walked stiffly to the tarmac. Kai loitered, but in a way that would not have seemed out of place.

"There's a place," Kai said quietly, "where you might be able to hire a temporary replacement for your crew."

Torri didn't respond. She instead watched Kai's face, seeing traces of the past there, flashes of a night spent in need and understanding.

"Ornin's," Kai said after a few seconds. "West on Mineway. Maybe ten minutes walking. I've heard it's a popular spot for traders. Especially later. Around twenty-one hundred or so is when things pick up." Her expression remained cool and professional but her eyes told a different story. Or so Torri hoped. She clung, once again, to a subtext, even as she nodded in acknowledgment.

Kai held Torri's gaze a second longer before she, too, exited the ship and she and the two guards began walking toward the next docking bay. Torri stared after them, heart thudding in her chest like a clock, hoping—*yes*. Kai glanced back over her shoulder, masking the motion with a surveil of Torri's ship.

Torri entered the door closing sequence on the panel and waited for it to return to its position, shaken at how she had reacted to seeing Kai, to being so near her. Ornin's. Would Kai go? Or was it a set-up of some sort? No, in spite of their political differences, Kai always operated with integrity, even when presented with every opportunity to do otherwise. She'd held Torri's secret this long, after all.

Torri returned to the bridge, busying herself with things her hands and brain did automatically, even as Kai filled her mind's eye, and Torri thought about the first time she'd ever seen her normally contemplative and almost taciturn Academy roommate smile.

She jerked her concentration back to the present and recorded Kai's inspection into the ship's log but she ended up thinking more about Kai's smile. They'd been bunked together for nearly two months. Their seminar and training schedules weren't in sync that first stretch, so they only saw each other in the mornings and late at night before bed. Torri had returned to their quarters from a particularly grueling day, completely spent and somewhat testy. She entered, just wanting to go to bed, and Kai looked up from her bunk, where she'd been reading through a training manual. Without a word, she got up and from beneath her mattress pulled a sleek black flask that she offered to Torri.

Both shocked and amused, Torri had accepted. She unscrewed the top and sniffed. Ryzin Solstice. She took a swallow and when finished, she looked at Kai and said, "Honey, I didn't know you cared," with a flippant little edge. And that's when Kai smiled. It pulled the right side of her mouth up, swirled through her eyes, and lit up her face. As well as something in the pit of Torri's stomach.

Torri pushed the memory to the back of her mind and finished with the bridge. The chronometer registered less than two hours to meet Jindor. Something else to ponder. She glared at nothing, seeking focus or perhaps clarity. After a few minutes, she had the former. The latter, however, eluded her. She set to work on a more thorough examination of the ship's hydraulic system, ballast, and thruster calibration. By the time she'd worked her way to the cargo bay, Jann and Saryl returned.

"So we had an inspection." Jann leaned on the doorjamb as Saryl looked over his shoulder.

Torri wiped her hands on the cloth she was carrying. "It went well. And you?" She ran her fingers over the control panel, activating several layers of jamming equipment and a feedback loop through the ship's comm system. She hated talking about business when docked, but it couldn't be helped in this instance. She moved to the doorway, so the three of them were barely a foot apart.

"Not good," Jann said in a low voice. "They've got Vintooth on near-lockdown. Where's the product?"

Torri leaned in closer. "There's a holding gallery inside, associated with the on-site workshop. Newburg mines like to have those, so each matrix has its distinctive type." Torri finished with the cloth and stuffed it halfway into her right front trousers pocket. "Did you see any traffic entering the mine that might have looked like a trader?"

"Yes. Once. Accompanied, of course."

"Of course. The Coalition is nothing if not thorough," Torri said dryly.

"Did the inspection crew leave us anything?" Saryl raised her eyebrows in a conspiratorial question.

"Images. Make sure what we have on board matches what they were wearing." Torri paused then grinned along with Jann. "But in the dust, we might be able to get away with a lot more."

"Thank Cyllea I gave up a life of leisure for this," Saryl said, laughter in her tone. "And when will we visit the Vintooth workshops?"

"Tomorrow. Eighteen hundred."

"I'll make arrangements." Jann nodded once and moved his broad frame past Saryl.

"And I'll get our wardrobes ready." Saryl winked and moved past Torri to another hidden compartment in the cargo bay, this one beneath a floor panel near the rear entrance.

Torri tossed the rag into a cleaning bin. "I'm off to see if there's a different way to acquire our tools," she said as Saryl extracted the case that held three Coalition guard uniforms from the hiding place.

"Do you want a curfew?" Saryl shot a mocking glance over her shoulder.

Torri rolled her eyes. "You and Dal take turns, if you need to avail yourself of the local entertainment."

"It's his night to carouse." Saryl affected a plaintive tone, but her eyes sparked in amusement. "But there're always the guards . . ."

"And that Miridian I told you about."

Saryl shook her head and gained her feet. "I'm not that desperate." She hefted the case. "Yet."

Torri laughed and left the cargo bay. She retrieved her goggles from the hook near the side entrance and looped them over her neck and entered the sequence to open the door. Once on the tarmac within the hangar, Jann closed the door, throwing her a wave and a grin. She waved back and left the docking bays, offering polite greetings to the Coalition guards she passed on her way to the outside world.

## CHAPTER 7

Torri found a table in Shintal's about midway between the front and the back. She sat in one of the chairs and ordered a bottle of local liqueur, two glasses, and some food. The bottle and glasses arrived first, and Torri poured herself a serving in one. Just as she set the bottle on the table, Jindor appeared. She slid into the seat on Torri's left.

"It's true," Jindor said, leaning close to Torri's ear. "This shirt looks good on you." She smiled. "But it would look better on my floor."

Torri picked the bottle up again and served Jindor. "I'm sure." She set the bottle to the side. "So who are you today?"

Jindor took a sip from the glass before answering. "Just a trader like yourself. Looking to make a few credits." She placed her glass on the table. "I have to make a run to Shanlin. Do you know it?"

Ice collected in Torri's throat, worked its way into her veins. A hoverdroid arrived with the small plates of food she had ordered. Numb, she slid her ID stick into its side as Jindor removed the dishes from its tray and arranged them on the table, within easy distance of them both.

"Possibly," Torri said, the word rough in her mouth. "It seems familiar." She reached for a puff pastry on a plate near Jindor's hand, fighting an urge to bolt into the evening winds.

"How familiar?" Jindor's gaze hardened, eyes like cold green fire in a pure-color black opal.

Torri chewed slowly, swallowed. "I lost a relative there. In the final battles before the collapse."

Jindor leaned a little closer. "Your relative's name?"

Torri shook her head slowly, tension wrapping around her spine. She fought it. "Not something I wish to discuss. Those times are over and I prefer to let the dead rest." She watched Jindor's face, trying to ascertain how this game might play out.

"Torri Rendego," Jindor said so quietly that Torri hoped she'd misheard. "That was her name."

Torri clenched her jaw so hard it hurt.

"I lost someone, too," Jindor continued. "Aylin ri' Til." She picked up her glass and took a drink then sat gazing into the blue liquid. "And things haven't been the same since."

Torri stared at the tabletop. She'd buried that identity in the swamps of Shanlin, when a slew of Coalition fighter vessels blew hers out of the sky. *The entire province crawled with them. Like maggots on a corpse.* Her final stand, that night. Coalition forces overwhelmed the rebel squadrons with sheer force of numbers, and one by one, they picked her back-up off. Torri was a skilled pilot but her true expertise was marksmanship, and she took dozens with her before a lucky pulsar missile crippled her starboard thrusters. She lost her ballast systems and with those, her ability to maneuver.

She remembered the smell of molten metal and hydraulic fluids, something like charred fish and hair. She couldn't get her fighter's systems to respond. She'd had to do a manual override while plummeting and careening toward the planet's surface. Finally the hatch blew, and air blasted across her helmet and facemask. But she waited. Waited until she was so close to the surface that she probably could have survived a fall without a parachute, if she hit water. The force of the ejection and the night air ripped breath from her lungs, and she struggled to maintain consciousness, free-falling for a few seconds in the darkness before she triggered her chute. Her ship exploded on impact, its demise lighting the dense swamplands and jungle below and debris shot past her like tracer fire.

Torri's thigh muscles contracted under the table, an involuntary response as she relived the fall, braced for the impact of the trees. She remembered thinking that she might yet not survive, might slam against a branch and fall, broken, to the canopy floor where animals would finish her off. Another unnamed casualty in the Coalition coup. Miraculously, she had slid between trees, and her chute caught, jerking her hard enough to snap her harness clips. But her hands gripped the broken straps, reacting on instinct, years of rigorous Academy training speeding her reflexes.

She had swung then, back and forth, like a pendulum, waiting a few minutes, determining damage to herself, before she brought herself to a stop using a tree branch. Torri climbed up to where the heliskin of her parachute had caught and extricated it so she could detach it from its cords and salvage what she could of the rigging before she figured out what to do next, a downed pilot in unknown territory.

Jindor's hand on hers retrieved her from her memories. "I needed to be sure," she said, gently squeezing Torri's fingers. "I remember your squadron. I coordinated Raptor and Seeker Wings."

Torri stared at her. "Tell me something only she would know," she said in a tone sharp enough to cut.

Jindor released Torri's hand. "She called her ship Vegas, and her commlink name that night was Spirit. The night before, her commlink name was Jester. And the night before that, it was Blade." She paused. "Her ship went down over Mangone Swamp. I lost its tracker connection at oh-two-hundred-nineteen hours."

Torri studied Jindor's face for a few moments. "Aylin's commlink name was Empress that night." That's why Jindor's voice had sounded familiar, somehow, when she approached Torri at the bar, though her accent was stronger now. She had probably worked to get rid of most of it when she ran squadrons. Torri had never seen her. The Resistance operated on a need-to-know basis, and Torri often hadn't known what her wingmates looked like. Another precaution, if an individual was captured.

Jindor speared a chunk of meat with a skewer. "And the night before that?"

"Bliss."

Jindor chewed the meat then swallowed, a faint smile on her lips. "Something in short supply since then."

Torri refilled their glasses and raised hers in a toast. "Well met."

Jindor acknowledged with a nod. "You're too fine-tuned to be Coalition," she said before she took a drink. She lowered her glass. "Too independent."

"I've been told that all my life." Torri spooned a mixture of meat and spices onto a flat piece of bread, relaxing a bit.

"Too fine-tuned for someone who's been a life-long trader, as well." Jindor picked up a puff pastry. "And you sounded familiar."

"As did you." Torri took a bite, watching Jindor's face for anything that would betray her as Coalition.

"I couldn't figure out where I'd heard you. After all, you allegedly didn't survive Shanlin. But then you pinned me that first night before I had time to consider such a possibility and I decided you weren't Coalition and you most likely had gotten training before the Collapse. So I figured you might be Academy and, at the very least, like-minded. I went through my memories and finally found the right context." She flashed a little smile and reached for a piece of flatbread.

"Your business in Newburg?" Torri watched Jindor place meat and roasted bril seeds on the bread.

"Same as you, I suspect. Trader." She put an old Empire inflection on the word, which added an underlying meaning, signaling that Jindor ran black markets as well as legitimate. Typical of so many rebels who survived the Collapse. They disappeared into the fissures that opened in the coup, adopting twilight identities, skirting borders between legal and illegal.

"Your business with Majan?"

Jindor finished chewing and swallowed. "Extra money. I base in Newburg, though it seems I'll have to reconsider that, with all the extra attention."

Torri reached for a plate near Jindor's right elbow. "Lucky, that. To have a base." She appreciated old Empire as much for its versatility across quadrants as for the different meanings one could inject into words and phrases with subtle intonations. She accented the first part of the word for "base," letting the rest drop, in direct contradiction to its preferred pronunciation.

Jindor's expression hardened again in recognition of Torri's insult. "I understand the need to test," she said. "Things revealed often create fear."

Torri raised a shoulder in a shrug. "What do you want from me?"

"A shared moment. And employment."

Torri studied her, fingers poised over the food.

"I have certification on class two and three light cargo vessels as well as class nine standard. And you already know I coordinate flight plans and formations. I don't need to tell you the types of navigational skills that requires." She tinged her words with the barest hint of sarcasm, something recognizable in any language.

Torri withdrew her fingers from the plate. "My apologies. I don't know your circumstances and I've made some assumptions."

"Accepted. And my apologies for treading in places I perhaps should not have."

"Sometimes circumstances offer no alternative." Torri picked up her glass and drained the last bit of liquid in it. "Now about your offer." She set her glass on the table. "You understand my reticence."

"Some kind of test, then."

Torri ran her fingers along the rim of the glass. "Perhaps." She looked up. "Do you have a ship?"

"No longer. I run with Majan's crews as required. I have other clients, as well."

Good. Nothing traceable, then. Torri nodded thoughtfully. "Get me into Vintooth tomorrow afternoon. Merchant credentials, Vector Quadrant."

Jindor took another bite of her flatbread before she answered, and Torri scanned the crowd. Boisterous miners, a few prostitutes of all persuasions, gamblers, outlaws. And a few Torri was certain were off-duty Coalition. A familiar form near the entrance caught her eye. Cyr, talking to an Earthman. Torri watched the exchange until a group of miners blocked it from her line of sight. Whatever Cyr was doing, it didn't involve brainjacking, for once. Was he looking for work? One of the miners moved, and she saw Cyr nod and pass something to the Earthman. Payment? Cyr slipped out the door, and Torri considered following him but decided the Earthman was a better avenue, especially since he headed for the card table.

"And what's in this for me?" Jindor said, bringing Torri back to the conversation.

"A cut of the profits. And, depending on how you perform with me and my crew, a job."

Jindor's eyes narrowed.

"You're coming with us into Vintooth." Torri reached for the bottle and poured another three fingers of liqueur into her glass. "So best get some credentials for yourself as well. Merchant's assistant."

Jindor raised an eyebrow. "You're Academy. Definitely. Am I right?"

Torri didn't reply, instead took a sip from her glass.

Jindor picked up her own glass, and Torri placed a microcomm on the table next to Jindor's right hand.

"That's my offer," Torri said as she stood, carrying her glass. "And if it works, and my crew takes to you . . ." She smiled. "Consider yourself hired." She raised her glass in a toast. "Docking bay fifteen, twelve hundred hours."

Jindor stifled a grin and toasted her back. Torri winked and moved off into the crowd toward the gaming table. Perhaps they'd find a navigator in Newburg after all.

She checked the chronometer above the door. A couple of hours before she'd head to Ornin's. The thought fluttered in her gut, like ash in a wind. The conversation with Jindor had unsettled her in some respects, and she needed Kai's solidity and presence, no matter the chasm between them, or the two years since she'd last seen her.

Torri wasn't in the mood to gamble, but observing a game might tell her a few things about the Earthman she'd seen talking to Cyr. She stood to his left, watching his face and how he held the cards in his hands. The hands of a miner. Thick-fingered, callused, decorated with scars and a fresh slice on his left thumb. *Good. Not Coalition, then.* Still, he could be an informant. She crossed her arms over her chest and filmed him with the recorder Jann had rigged in her wrist reader.

*Never assume people are what you see on the surface. Observe, remember, and place it all in a bigger context.* Another instructor's voice from her past, conducting a training session on reconnaissance. *Everything is part of larger patterns. Learn the rhythms of those patterns.* She continued studying the game, looking like nothing more than an interested player herself, watching techniques.

The Earthman's bland, broad face betrayed nothing. He'd

been playing a while, obviously. But he played conservatively. Not much money to spare and not a gambler. Just here to spend some time and unwind. What, then, did he want with the likes of Cyr? Or vice-versa? Torri watched his play. He won two hands, then lost one. At that point he withdrew from the game and went to cash in his winnings. When he finished with that, he stopped to talk to a group of men drinking and chatting near the main bar. A few minutes later he worked his way out of Shintal's, Torri behind him. Once outside, he headed toward the mines.

*Going to work, possibly.* She maintained about twenty paces between them, and the busy street offered more cover for her. A rare break from the wind, and Newburg's topside pulsed with life and laughter. Typical of dry climates, the summer night descended with a slight chill, offering a bit of relief from the brutal blast furnace days, though by dawn the air would be well on its way to hot again.

Torri hung back as her quarry approached the mine entrance. He went through the security check into the mine's interior. Perhaps Cyr was arranging his own business? He needed money to feed his habit, at the very least. The miner might be on the take at work, and Cyr wanted access to stones. Or the miner could be an informant. Cyr's addiction left no room for integrity. She commed Saryl.

"Syl."

"You'll be interested to know I saw a former acquaintance of ours out and about."

Pause. "Were you able to speak with him?"

Torri started walking away from the mines, keeping to busy thoroughfares. "No. But he was speaking with someone else who might be trouble." She sent the image to Saryl from her wrist unit.

"I'll see what I can find out."

"Thanks. Oh, we may have a replacement for our former acquaintance."

"Really. Care to elaborate?" Saryl's tone was droll.

"Tomorrow."

"Intriguing. Looking forward to it."

"While you're doing that, run the name Jindor Korickis." She lowered her voice a notch. "And while you're at it, run Aylin ri' Til."

"Even more intriguing. Out."

Torri closed the link. Saryl had ensured that Cyr left the ship for the last time with an extra accessory attached to the charm necklace he always wore, since wiping him from the ship's memory automatically wiped formal tracking devices that the crew carried. The energy generated by his motions kept the informal one charged and broadcasting.

The past two days he'd been frequenting jackdens. No surprise there, but Saryl had noticed a break in that pattern yesterday, when his signal appeared near a Coalition barracks. Which didn't necessarily mean that and what Torri saw at Shintal's were related. But the prickling on the back of her neck told her the two incidents probably had something to do with each other. She sighed as she walked. Sometimes this line of work was just too slagging complicated.

## CHAPTER 8

Torri found Ornin's twenty minutes later and she took a position across the way from the crowded eatery near an outdoor bar, observing the clientele that entered and exited. Kai was right. Mostly traders. A few miners and jackers as well, but nothing that she wouldn't expect at an eating establishment in a city like this.

An all-too familiar figure approached the entrance from the east. Kai was out of uniform, dressed in dark trousers and shirt. She hesitated at the entrance to Ornin's and scanned the street. Torri made no move to dodge Kai's recon. Instead, she welcomed it, welcomed the memories that accompanied it. Kai eventually saw her, as Torri knew she would. Kai always could pick her out of a crowd.

Torri watched, her heart in her throat, as Kai waited a few moments before she crossed the street, gaze locked with hers. Kai was off-duty. Which meant she would speak freely. About what, Torri didn't know. Ultimately, it didn't matter. She'd take whatever time Kai offered. A thought as unsettling as it was honest.

Kai joined her near the bar. She hooked her thumbs on her belt, something she did when she wasn't sure what direction a conversation would take. "Syl," she said tentatively. Trying the name out, like a new word in a language she was just learning. She leaned closer. "Have you some time?"

Torri smiled, incapable of doing much else, this close to her. *For you, as much as you'll take.* "I do."

"Walk with me?"

Torri studied Kai's face for a long moment, wondering at this approach, wary about the quiet urgency in her tone and all too cognizant of the divide between them. *She's out of uniform.* Torri nodded once, and Kai relaxed, visible in the way her right shoulder dipped as well as in the expression in her eyes. She turned and moved into the street. Torri followed, staying close as they walked. Twice Kai slowed, and her hand brushed Torri's both times, something Torri knew wasn't accidental. Kai was never careless with her movements.

Kai weaved through the throngs, Torri close behind her, admiring the way Kai's trousers fit and her familiar gait. Pragmatic, sensible, crisp. She led Torri back to a main thoroughfare that skirted the edge of the closest mine. Work never stopped here, and a haze of dust obscured the lights at the entrance. Torri felt rather than heard the hum and throb of heavy machinery beneath her boots.

They passed the southern entrances of the mines, and Kai turned right back into Newburg, down another busy side street that Torri didn't recognize. Clearly a vendors' paradise. Incense and local hash, pungent but not unpleasant, accosted her as they made their way through the raucous gatherings. Music that reminded her of some of the forbidden places she frequented as a Cadet mixed with the ebb and flow of many voices, many accents. An oddly rhythmic and poetic harmony.

Kai began working her way to the left, between tents and booths, until she came to an alleyway with barely enough room for a single human to negotiate without turning sideways. Torri instinctively held back. Kai turned, a question in her eyes. At Torri's expression, she leaned close, near Torri's ear.

"I have to be careful." Her unspoken *"Please trust me"* hung on the end of the statement.

Torri nodded again, and Kai squeezed her forearm, leading her down the alleyway until she came to a heavy wooden door on the right. She knocked twice, waited a beat, knocked twice more. The door opened, and a tall, thin Miridian dressed in a black robe stood looking at them impassively. Male, Torri gauged. He appraised her then shifted his gaze to Kai. Without a word, he moved aside, and Kai entered. Torri followed, and the Miridian shut the door behind them. They stood in a cramped foyer, glow sockets providing barely enough light for Torri to distinguish the entranceway to a ramp behind his lanky figure.

"Well met," Kai said softly in Empire, inclining her head slightly to the left.

"One hopes." He waved a taloned hand toward the ramp behind him, and Kai brushed past him, glancing over her shoulder to make sure Torri followed her. A hundred paces later, walking in silence and even worse lighting than the room before, they emerged into a gallery busy with Newburg's night shift denizens and vendors. Here, however, Torri recognized the energy of black market business and entertainment, something the Coalition would never allow. At least not openly. She threw a glance at Kai, mildly surprised that she would frequent such a place, even off-duty. But she'd been here before, by the way she headed through the crowd.

Torri kept pace with her, noise assaulting her ears. As loud now as it might be during the day, voices and music bounced off the cavern's ceiling. Roasted spiced meat, hasha, and the sour smell of mashed croll berries mixed with the odors of many bodies accompanied them as Kai guided them through the crowd. She led Torri to another corridor stuffed with rug and furniture merchants, shouting good-natured insults about each other's tapestries and fabrics. The crush of the crowd forced Kai to slow her pace, and much to Torri's surprise and pleasure, she twined her fingers with Torri's. The touch sent flares shooting through Torri's gut and down her thighs. Kai retained her hold and pulled her along, tightening her grip. A few minutes passed as they patiently worked their way through the throngs toward the opposite side of the corridor.

Kai pulled Torri into what seemed to be an eatery carved into the rock, where she waited. Torri's boots sank into thick rugs and what light the glow sockets offered was set much lower than standard. Kai nodded at the host, an Earthman, who nodded back and made no further effort at communication. Kai released Torri's hand and led her to a low-slung table in a back alcove, clearly designed for use while sitting on the many cushions that surrounded it.

Kai removed her boots, and Torri did the same as Kai drew the filmy red curtain across the alcove's entrance. Torri took a seat on the cushions, leaning back against the wall, surface chiseled smooth and cool. It offered stability, something she needed at the moment, as she faced Kai.

"Are you hungry?" Kai waited by the curtain.

Torri bit back the tease that rose unbidden to her lips and instead replied, "No, thanks. Not thirsty, either."

Kai's fingers fell from the fabric, and she removed a jammer from her cargo pocket. Torri did the same. Kai triggered it and placed the device on the table, and Torri set hers next to it. Kai then settled herself cross-legged on a cushion opposite Torri. She ran both hands through her hair and sat for a moment, gathering her thoughts. Torri knew not to interrupt when Kai was preparing a statement. Her gut churned.

"Your man Cyr is selling information to the Coalition," Kai finally said, using his real name. She raised her gaze to Torri's. "And it's not favorable toward you. I'm supposed to put you under heavier surveillance."

Torri clenched then unclenched her jaw. "How bad is it?"

"Not very, yet. He hasn't said who your client is or who you've contracted with here."

"That's because he doesn't know."

A tiny smile caught the edge of Kai's mouth. "I figured as much."

Torri shrugged. "Do you have someone on him?"

"No. He's been coming to the Coalition."

Torri's brow furrowed in puzzlement. Kai wasn't referring to the Coalition as "us." Perhaps she was worried about eavesdropping? No, they both had jammers operating. What, then? "He's gaming us both." She rearranged herself and pulled a commdisk out of her pocket. She put it on the table, and Kai picked it up and slid it into her wrist reader. After a few minutes, she looked up at Torri.

"Who is he?"

"Don't know yet. But Cyr's either paying him or providing him information. He's not Coalition, then?"

Kai ran a check on the man's image and biometrics. "No." She removed the commdisk and handed it back to Torri. "But I can't run a deeper check when I'm off-duty unless I file a report as to why I had to do so."

Torri didn't miss the sarcasm in her tone. "He's affiliated with the mines somehow," she said. "But I don't know what the capacity is. I thought he might be a Coalition informant, but if he's not coming up as that—"

"Not right off, but that doesn't mean he's not." She locked her gaze with Torri's. "Certain Coalition officials aren't entirely immune to greed. And they like to know who's running checks on informants," she added cryptically.

Torri nodded. Kai couldn't risk running afoul of those officials. It must have been frustrating for her, trying to do her job with the integrity and ability Torri knew Kai always employed, and the very people she was supposed to serve were black-marketing with the people she was charged to bring in.

Kai sucked air between her teeth and sat back, leaning against the wall. "Is your man slagging you, then?"

Torri sighed. "Probably. Or he might just want some action. Or maybe both. We've been monitoring him." She regarded Kai, searching for echoes of the night they shared in Hallifin.

She found them in Kai's eyes, but they dissipated as quickly as they'd come. No matter. She raised an eyebrow. "How's your family?"

Kai stared at her, taken aback. "Why?"

"Because I suspect that has some bearing on why you're here with me."

"Damn you," Kai said, though she laughed softly. "I don't see you for a while and I forget how well you know me."

"It's mutual."

A silence descended between them, heavy with the past. Kai broke it. "Not as well as they could be."

*Getting fucked by the Coalition, no doubt.* "There's a market squeeze on here. Did you know?" Kai's upper lip twitched. No, she clearly hadn't known. "Why do you think you're here?" Torri pressed. "The Coalition wants to keep stones from leaving Newburg, either legitimately or not. Somebody's cornering. I'm not sure who, but whoever it is has Coalition pull."

Kai sucked her lower lip between her teeth and released it as she leaned forward. "You're sure?"

Torri gave her a "you need to ask?" look.

She sighed at Torri's expression. "Of course you are."

"And you've no doubt already broken up a few smuggling groups." Torri paused. "I haven't seen Krayden here."

Kai rolled her eyes. "Shut him down last week."

"Vortal?"

"On the run. He got wind of the crackdown and hasn't shown up."

"Jef Mar's crew?"

Kai grimaced. "Now *he's* been slick. I haven't found him yet, but I picked up his second-in-command three days ago."

Torri smiled wryly. "And me?"

Kai's jaw clenched. "I'm not looking for you."

"Obviously not right now, since you're off-duty—"

"Ever." The word bore baggage and hope as she said it,

and Torri winced inwardly at what it cost Kai to acknowledge it.

She reached across the table and took one of Kai's hands in her own. "What's going on with your family?"

Shadows flickered through Kai's eyes. "Things I probably should have noticed years ago." Her gaze fell on their hands, but she didn't pull away. "Things you said about the Coalition before we graduated." She tightened her hold, and a warmth Torri hadn't experienced since Hallifin coursed up her arm into her chest. "They own me," Kai said softly, bitterness curling the edges of the statement.

"Tell me." Torri stroked Kai's fingers, wanting nothing more than to take her into her arms and never let go.

Kai shook her head. "It's always about money. Another damn tax, masquerading as a 'security fee.' Or some slag-assed official demanding 'protection tithes.'" She caught Torri's gaze. "I should have listened to you."

"How much?"

Kai made a noise deep in her throat, almost like a growl. "It's not something that can be fixed with a lump sum." She exhaled, frustrated. "The Coalition has decided, in its infinite wisdom, to appropriate half my family's holdings as a military base. And we are, of course, invited to pay for this exquisite privilege." She practically spat the last part. They sat for a bit until Kai spoke again, stubborn. "I don't want your money."

"I know." Torri continued to stroke Kai's fingers, calling on every deity she could think of to let her keep doing it, to keep Kai from reclaiming her hand.

"I'm too visible now," Kai said. "I can't leave. And if I could, what in the name of Cyllea would I do? At least I have some sway over the taxes they demand, given my rank. And my service to the cause." She glared at the wall behind Torri's head. "I won't let them have the holdings. I can't."

"How much longer do you have?"

"They're negotiating"—she said it sarcastically—"now. I'm putting them off as long as I can. I expect that within another month or two, I'll have to accept whatever deal they offer." The pain and anger in her voice were palpable.

"Why did they choose *your* family's holdings?" Torri adjusted her position, needing to move her leg but not wanting to release Kai's hand.

"Available water and an expanse of desert for training flights."

"There's plenty of desert on Earth. Why yours?"

"I don't fucking know." Kai used her free hand to rub her forehead.

"Think. Has anyone in your family chafed a Coalition official?"

Kai looked up. "You think that's what this is about? Something that trivial?"

"It's no different than local Empire regents getting tweaked about some perceived slight. The difference then was that the oversight courts worked. Now they're packed with Coalition lackies."

Kai didn't respond right away.

"Or is there something about your land that makes it worth the Coalition's while to appropriate it? Mineral wealth? Strategic location?" *A like-mind uprising, perhaps?*

"I've considered those possibilities. There's more mineral wealth in other parts of the area that are easier to acquire than my family's holdings. And yes, I am exploring rumors of a rebellion," she said, as if reading Torri's thoughts.

"Rumors don't require land appropriation. When did they start?"

"Don't know for sure. Last year, it seems. Meli notified me. She said she'd heard something from a Coalition soldier who got a little too drunk before she took him to bed."

"Your sister always did like a challenge," Torri said, offering a little smile.

Kai shook her head with frustration, but returned the smile. "Which is why our father married her off when he did. Though that doesn't seem to have stopped her appetites."

Torri shrugged. "Marriage is most often an economic arrangement. You yourself said that Meli's husband has his own appetites he feeds on the side."

"True, though they like each other well enough. And he's shrewd about politics, making all the right overtures to all the right people."

"Have you considered him, then, as a reason that the Coalition is interested in your holdings? Perhaps he's playing politics, using the rumors as fuel. People have allied for less."

Kai's jaw muscles clenched, and she was silent for a moment. When she spoke, angry resignation marked her tone. "I suppose I didn't want to believe you before the Collapse." She muttered something under her breath that sounded like a profanity.

"Not many did," Torri said, tone gentle.

"But you were one of the few."

Torri smiled. "I've always had a problem with authority. You know that."

Kai stared at her then smiled back, and Torri's breathing sped up. "True," Kai said, laughing softly. "It certainly wasn't out of character for you to rebel."

"And you were surprised that I did?" Torri tested the boundaries between them.

"No. Disappointed." She tempered her response by pulling Torri's hand to her mouth. Kai ran her lips lightly over Torri's fingertips, and fire engulfed Torri's bones. "I didn't want to lose you," Kai said as she returned Torri's hand to the table without letting go. "I thought I did, when I heard what happened at Shanlin. They said you were dead, and for a year I believed that." She moved her hand, adjusting its position so she could stroke Torri's palm with her thumb. "When you sent word to me . . ." She trailed off.

"I wanted you to know," Torri said, marveling at the sudden urge to cry. "Just you."

"Why? We chose such different paths."

"No. The paths chose us. We were a team. I never forgot that." *We still are, though you refuse to accept it.*

"I was so glad you were alive. But I also wanted to kick your rebellious ass, putting me through that for a year."

"Cut me a little slack," Torri said, half-teasing. "It wasn't like I could just access Academy databases and find you."

Kai pinched the bridge of her nose with the thumb and index finger of her free hand. "I almost died myself, thinking you were gone."

Hope filled Torri's chest. "I found you. Twice."

"Three times." Kai lowered her hand from her face. "Here we are, after all." And it was the Kai from their Academy days that regarded her from across the table, the quiet, stoic Cadet whose occasional smiles broke through her serious demeanor and lit wildfires in Torri's heart, sent need and desire to bed with her on more nights than she could count, staring in frustration through the dark of their shared quarters at Kai's sleeping form. How many times she'd wanted to bridge the gulf between their bunks, press herself against Kai's back, and rest her lips on the skin of Kai's neck. How many times she'd stopped herself, only to battle the urge again the next night. And the next. And the next after that.

"You found *me* this time," Torri said, placing an inflection on her phrasing that connoted far more than the statement itself.

Kai smiled, and the divide between them shrank. "How much longer do you need here?"

"We can leave tomorrow night, should all go smoothly."

"And if it doesn't?"

Torri raised an eyebrow. "You doubt my abilities?"

"I've never doubted you. 'But in the absence of static circumstances'—"

"'Every contingency must be considered,'" Torri finished. "I hated that seminar. Nothing but theorizing."

"You always did prefer a more action-oriented approach." Kai squeezed her hand.

"You helped me pass that damn session. Drilling all those theories into my head."

"It was hard work," Kai said in a long-suffering tone. "If you hadn't passed, I'd never have heard the end of it."

"Some things never change. You'll never hear the end of it if we don't get out of here in a timely fashion. We'll be gone no later than twenty-two hundred." *But the stakes are much higher now than just a mark on a progress record.*

"I'll do what I can."

"I know." Torri studied their hands, still clasped together on the table. "Do you get any flying in?"

"No." Kai's response carried frustration and resignation.

"Why not? You're one of the best. Why don't they use the skills you have?"

Kai shrugged.

"Do you want to?"

"Every damn day." Kai tilted her head back and stared at the ceiling. "Every damn day," she repeated softly.

Torri took Kai's other hand. "Come with me."

Kai tightened her grip on Torri's hands. "I can't. You know that."

"Because of what? Your work? Your rank?"

Kai looked away.

"Your family?"

"I can't," she said again so softly that Torri wasn't sure she actually heard it.

"All of those, then."

The muscles in Kai's jaw bunched then released.

"We can arrange things," Torri pushed. "And you'd fly again."

Kai focused on her at that, regret and longing clouding her features. "I don't know if I can live like you. In the shadows. Always on the run."

"It's not like that. Not always."

"How, then?" Kai stroked the backs of Torri's hands with her thumbs. "How many identities do you have? You have to make sure they don't ever find out who you really are, what you did, and what you're doing now. Is that a life? Are you free?"

Torri slowly pulled her hands from Kai's, the questions roiling in her gut. "Yes. And yes," she said, a chill in her tone that left her throat cold. She unfolded her legs from under the table, reached for her jammer, and stood. "I'm free in the knowledge that what I'm doing is forced upon me by circumstances I fought to prevent." She slid the jammer into her pocket and started putting her boots on, wanting to be gone from here, from the sense of loss that thickened the air between them and left a hole in the middle of her chest. Kai watched her, silent.

"Freedom is ten percent reality and ninety percent perception." Torri shifted her weight onto her left leg, shoving her foot the rest of the way into her boot. "What is *your* ratio?" She stood staring at Kai for a long moment, aching to throw herself across the table and show Kai exactly how she felt about her, as fucking stubborn as Kai could be. Instead, she reached for the curtain.

"Don't go."

Torri's fingers hovered at the edge of the fabric, a delicate barrier between their shared history and the world beyond.

"Please."

Torri lowered her arm, waiting.

Kai retrieved the remaining jammer, got up, and put her own boots on. When she finished, she straightened and moved closer, close enough to reach out and run her fingers along

Torri's left arm, up to her shoulder, where Kai's hand stopped, the heat from her palm soaking through Torri's shirt to her skin.

"I'm sorry," Kai whispered. She moved her hand to Torri's face and cupped her cheek. "I'm so sorry."

Torri leaned into Kai's touch, unable to resist, knowing she wouldn't if given a choice.

"Will you—?" Kai started.

"Yes."

Kai brushed a kiss across Torri's lips, an all too brief recognition of what bound them together and what also kept them apart. Kai stepped back, a smile playing along the curve of her upper lip. She pushed the fabric aside and exited the alcove, Torri right behind her, breathing matching the pounding of her heart and the pulsing much deeper than that.

Kai led her the few paces to the back of the eatery and through a curtain to a metal door that Kai triggered with a code on the keypad. They passed through into a narrow corridor tunneled into the rock that took them farther into the bowels of Newburg, doors set at intervals on either side. A residential stretch, Torri surmised. They passed five on the left and four on the right until Kai stopped at the sixth on the left and entered a number onto the keypad. The door slid open, and Kai went in first, then entered another code on the inside keypad that sealed the door behind them. Kai took her boots off and tossed them in a corner near the door.

Typical Kai, Torri thought, noting the simple furnishings. A low maroon couch and matching chair occupied a far corner and a small round table and two chairs claimed another corner. Rugs in solid, bright colors covered the stone floor, another of Kai's quirks. She gravitated toward earth tones but she loved splashes of color as a counterpoint. Also typical Kai, she chose living quarters as far away from her work as she could get, metaphorically and literally. She guarded her privacy fiercely, something Torri had learned about her quickly.

"How long have you been stationed in Newburg?"

Kai adjusted the light emanating from the glow sockets with a wave past the sensor and Torri smiled as Kai's body language broadcast relaxation.

"Three months now." Kai glanced over her shoulder. "Thirsty?"

"I'm hoping you haven't forgotten old habits and you have some of that tea you always made."

"No, I haven't forgotten." She regarded Torri. "That was your favorite." She broke the moment and disappeared through another curtain into an adjoining room and returned a few minutes later with two tall cylindrical glasses, one of which she handed to Torri. "Long life," she said, raising her empty palm toward Torri in the Cadet salute.

Torri touched her palm to Kai's. "Long life." She sipped, and the familiar flavor of jayfruit and Ceylon dark filled her mouth. She swallowed, savoring. "Better than I remember."

"I've experimented over the years." Kai raised an eyebrow sardonically at her.

"And it shows. Would you consider leaving your position and going into trading?" She was only partially teasing. "I have many clients who would sell extra limbs for this formula."

"Old family secret. Emphasis on 'secret.'" She winked and took another drink. "Besides, I don't need any more limbs."

Torri flashed a grin. She loved when Kai relaxed into herself, when she allowed a window of opportunity into some of her inner worlds. It had taken nearly a year at the Academy before she opened up with Torri, showing her a few pieces of her past. These Torri guarded as carefully as Kai, and over time Kai provided even more pieces, more glimpses, until by the time they graduated, Torri was almost a part of Kai's family.

And then everything changed.

The touch of Kai's fingers on her own pulled her back to the present.

"More?"

"No, not yet." She relinquished her empty glass to Kai, who took it and stood regarding her, worry etched into her forehead.

"Where did you go?"

Torri shook her head, gently dismissing the question. "Nowhere I needed to be."

Kai frowned, sighed, and retreated to the kitchen. Torri hesitated a second then followed, only to nearly run into Kai as she re-emerged. They stared at each other, unseen currents arced in the air between them, shooting like lightning down Torri's back. Kai closed the circuit, kissing Torri hard and deep, her hands on Torri's hips, pulling her close, and Torri responded with equal fervor, running her hands up Kai's back, then down to her belt.

Still kissing, she pulled Kai's shirt free of her trousers and somehow got the front clasps undone. Kai shrugged out of it with an urgency that fueled Torri's need and she unfastened her own clasps as Kai triggered the release on Torri's belt then on her own before focusing on Torri's underliner. She pulled it up and over Torri's head, and Torri's skin prickled as air coursed over her, no longer blocked by microthin fabric. Kai removed her own underliner before Torri could, tossing it aside with one hand while sliding her other arm around Torri and kissing her again, this time achingly slow, exquisitely tender, claiming Torri's lips and then her tongue with her own.

Torri sank into Kai's body heat, into the way their skin and the curves of their muscles fit together, and into the flare of a dream first shared in Hallifin. Somehow they made it to the sleeping room, up the two steps to the raised ledge on which Kai's bed rested. Wrapped in Kai's arms, Torri fell back onto the mattress, Kai's familiar body on hers, mouth coaxing heat from her neck and shoulders.

Abruptly, Kai stopped and gazed down at Torri. She kissed

her softly on the forehead and left the mattress. Torri propped herself on her elbows, a question forming on her lips. Kai smiled in the muted amber light from the glow sockets in the walls and pulled Torri's boots off, letting them fall to the floor below the ledge. She then turned her attention to Torri's trousers and underwear, removing them in one smooth motion as Torri arched her hips to help. Kai let those articles of clothing fall, as well, and she stood at the foot of the bed, vulnerability and something Torri didn't recognize on her features.

Torri moved to the end of the bed and seated herself there, feet on the floor. She pulled Kai toward her and undid her trousers. Kai wrapped the fingers of one hand in Torri's hair and with her other she traced circles between Torri's shoulder blades. Torri slowly worked Kai's pants past her hips and gently pressed her lips against Kai's abdomen, above the waistband of her underwear. Kai's fingers tightened in Torri's hair, and her breath hissed between her teeth. Torri circled Kai's navel with her tongue as she pulled Kai's pants down farther, to her knees. She ran her fingers up Kai's thighs, along the planes the hard muscles beneath her skin created, reveling in how that felt, in how doing so made her both weak and powerful.

Kai groaned, and Torri hooked her fingers onto the waistband of Kai's underwear and slowly pulled, easing the fabric down her hips, then farther. She kissed the boundary between flesh and hair, then tracked lower, the feel of Kai's dampness on her mouth and the heavy, rich smell of her arousal overwhelming her senses. For a moment, Torri couldn't breathe, couldn't move, couldn't even find the line between them, but it didn't matter because Kai stepped out of her clothing and pushed Torri gently back onto the bed, and something like magic bridged the choices they'd made, something like memories bound them together, but something more hovered in the spaces that merged between them.

Kai took her time at first, and Torri let her until Kai entered her, when the connection that coursed from Kai's fingers through the far corners of Torri's core sent them straining and gasping in a tangle of sweat-slicked limbs and skin across the mattress, Torri groaning a climax against Kai's shoulder, leaving a bruise. Hours might have passed. Maybe days, as Kai welcomed Torri's fingers and then tongue into her heat not once but many times, and she strained against her, digging her fingertips into Torri's back, burying her face where Torri's neck met her shoulder, leaving something that might have been tears.

Time's edges folded, joining past and present and for a while, the world was only the two of them and the future was whatever they made of it, until Torri collapsed against Kai for the third—or was it fourth?—time, nearly spent from their exertions, tingling and raw in places both physical and emotional. They lay thus, Torri listening to Kai breathe. She closed her eyes and thought maybe she heard Kai's heart beating.

Kai sighed contentedly and hugged Torri closer as she laughed softly. "You smell like me."

"I hope so, after what you just put me through." Torri nuzzled her neck.

"It's never enough," Kai said quietly.

Torri stopped what she was doing and looked at Kai's face, just visible in the room's lighting.

"After Hallifin, all I had was the commdisk you left." Kai stroked Torri's back. "I played it so much I nearly drove myself crazy. But I had to be sure that you really had been there, and that what I thought happened really did."

"Why didn't you contact me?"

"Why do you ask when you know the answer?" Kai brushed a lock of Torri's hair away from her forehead.

"Do you remember the day we finished our first year at the Academy?" Torri shifted the conversation. "Your last exam was scheduled late and you didn't get back until twenty-two hundred."

"I was so fucking tired. And I just *knew* you were going to have forty people stuffed into our quarters and I'd have to find a way to sleep in the midst of that. I dreaded going home that night. But Cyllea, I was ragged." She traced Torri's jaw with her fingertips. "And I walked in, expecting noise and drunken debauchery—"

"Not that there's anything wrong with that," Torri said, smiling.

"In moderation, one hopes." Kai kissed Torri's chin. "I walked in and . . . no revelry. Soft music and candles, of all things. I never did find out where you'd gotten those."

"I have my ways." Torri waggled her eyebrows.

"You still do." Kai smiled. "Oh, and food. And there you were, waiting. You asked me how it went and you made sure I ate and—" Her brow furrowed. "I don't even remember how I got to bed."

"On your own. I didn't take advantage of you. Though I *did* take your boots off and tuck you in."

"You didn't take advantage of me? Are you sure? I could have *sworn*—" Kai stopped, a full grin lighting her features.

Torri propped herself on her elbows and slid her left thigh between Kai's. "Okay, I'll confess. I kissed you that night. Once."

Kai raised her eyebrows, skeptical, still teasing.

"Fine. Twice. Once on the lips and once on the forehead. On my father's holding, it was just twice." Torri moved her thigh, gratified to hear Kai's low moan.

"Mmm." Kai closed her eyes and moved against Torri's thigh. "I know it was just twice," she said softly. "But I wanted more."

Torri adjusted her weight and ran her thumb over Kai's nipple. "Why didn't you say something?"

"You know some of the reasons." Kai arched into her touch.

"Family, duty, career. And me. Not quite your type." Torri leaned down and grazed Kai's other nipple with her teeth. "So you thought," she said before she took Kai's nipple into her mouth. Kai gasped, and Torri released her. "I didn't know," she said, watching Kai's eyes and aching anew in parts she didn't know she had.

"I didn't think you'd ever want someone like me."

Torri stared at her, the breath knocked from her lungs at this piece Kai showed her. "The first time I saw you smile," she finally managed, "was when I knew. And a few months after that I kissed you."

"But you didn't know much about me then," Kai challenged, though her breath had speeded up as she and Torri moved slowly together, Torri's thigh sliding through Kai's heat. "And you didn't do it again."

"Because you are who you are." Torri's own arousal soared. "And the more I found out about you, the more I just wanted to protect you, and provide my friendship. If I couldn't have what I really wanted from you, I'd learn to live with what you could offer." Fire built at her core, spread through her torso and down her legs. "And maybe I wanted you to see who I really am. You became too important." She groaned softly and stopped, trying to finish her thought. "You were too important then—as you are now—for anything less than everything I have to give."

They stared at each other, neither moving, and Torri's chest constricted with tears she wouldn't shed though she thought she saw them mirrored in Kai's eyes. Kai pulled her close.

"Torri," she said softly near her ear.

The sound of her name on Kai's lips opened doors within her she thought she'd locked, and an identity she'd left seven years ago in the Mangone swamp surfaced and washed through her like a tide.

Kai pressed her face to Torri's shoulder. "Torri," she said again, mouth grazing her skin. "How I've wanted to call you by your name, since I found out you were still alive." She kissed Torri's neck then stopped and regarded her for a long moment. "I haven't said your name since that day you sent word that you had survived Shanlin. Not even when we were together in Hallifin. But it's still like part of me has been missing without even your name as a connection."

"It's yours." Torri ran her fingertips over the scar on Kai's cheek. "That way, I'll know it's you contacting me. And I'll know to find you." She kissed Kai's forehead. "My offer will always stand. You're far too skilled a pilot not to fly. It's in your blood." Kai started to say something but Torri pressed her fingers against Kai's lips. "Please. Just let me leave the offer with you."

Kai hesitated then nodded and kissed Torri's fingertips before she once again began moving slowly against Torri's thigh. And Torri responded, losing herself in the warmth and safety she found in Kai's arms, in the hope she read in her eyes, and the possibility engendered in a name.

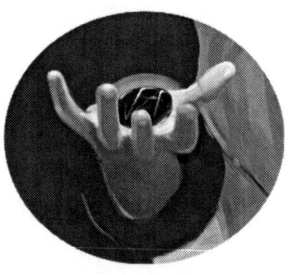

# CHAPTER 9

Torri woke with a jerk, Kai's hand over her mouth. An insistent beeping sounded in the outer room. The door signal. Kai removed her fingers from Torri's lips, urgency written across her features. She left the bed, motioning for Torri to follow her to the bathroom in the far corner of the sleeping room through a dark blue curtain. Kai turned on the water in the shower tube and entered, Torri behind her. A minute passed. Kai's commlink must have signaled because she mouthed a curse and left the shower, dripping. Torri turned the water off, waiting.

"Tinsdale." Kai stood outside the door, water running down her back and legs to pool beneath her feet. *A ruse*, Torri thought. Whoever was at the door would see that Kai had been in the shower and not think anything past that. Kai listened to whomever was talking for a while, placing a hand on her hip, tense. "I'm not on duty for two hours." She stalked out of the bathroom, trailing water, then reappeared and pointed at the tube. Torri nodded and remained where she was as Kai disappeared through the curtain again.

She listened, and after a few moments, she heard voices. She picked out Kai's, clipped and professional. A tinge of irritation in her tone. Then a male voice, almost apologetic. Another male voice, and then a female. Then Kai again. Torri strained and thought she caught "Vintooth" and "security" but she wasn't sure. Then silence.

Kai entered the bathroom a few moments later, wrapped in a thin robe. "There's been a security situation at Vintooth."

Torri waited, the set of Kai's jaw and mouth broadcasting her agitation.

"They've closed the main entrance to all but mining personnel and Coalition. And all ships registered to merchants and traders are under lockdown. Interrogations begin at fifteen hundred."

"What happened?"

"A tip," Kai said, tone cold. "Someone planning a theft."

*Cyr. Or worse, Jindor.* "Why traders and merchants? Why not everyone?"

"I don't know. I have to report now." She let the bathrobe fall and stepped back into the tube with Torri. She turned on the jet dry and warm air pulsed over Torri's skin and hair. She knew not to press Kai. The fragile truce they'd just begun constructing might not withstand demands for more information. She turned her back to Kai so the air could dry her front. To her amazement, Kai slid her arms around her waist from behind and held her tight, rocking slowly back and forth for a few moments before releasing her. She stepped out of the tube, catching Torri's gaze with her own, something wistful in her expression before she passed through the curtain into the sleeping room.

Torri turned the air off before leaving the bathroom. She found her trousers, underwear, blouse, and underlining on the bed, laid out for her. Kai's gesture settled with a strange warmth in her chest, a sign that Kai was maybe more comfortable with the intimacy they'd expressed, and she wanted to make it a pattern. Maybe.

Torri dressed, then watched Kai fasten the clasps on her grey uniform shirt, standing in front of a shallow closet. She tucked it into her trousers and threaded her belt through the thick loops at her waist. A pair of sleek black ultra-polished boots stood patiently nearby, and Kai pulled them on, arranging her pant legs within and drawing the straps on her boots tight. Precise and practiced. Like when she dressed for class.

"I didn't get a chance to congratulate you on your upcoming promotion," Torri said, gesturing at the stripes on Kai's left bicep as she approached. "When is it final?"

"Six months."

Torri smiled. "Will you perhaps get a better assignment?"

Kai looked up at her, an expression on her face that left Torri reeling. "This one has proven the best I've had." She smoothed the front of her shirt though it didn't need it.

They stood in silence until Torri reluctantly voiced what she'd dreaded to discuss. "If I get my crew out before the interrogations start, will we still be subject to security measures?"

"I doubt it. But I don't know. They're keeping this locked up tighter than usual," she said, a grimace on her lips. "Not that it matters. Somebody always finds out." Kai retrieved her pistol belt from her closet and positioned it around her waist, just below her other belt. She activated the magnetic buckle and adjusted the blaster in its holster, which she wore lower than her hip, then fastened the strap around her leg, just above her knee to hold it in place. Kai had always preferred to wear her weapons that way. She didn't like something riding high on her hip. "They're wanting us in full regalia," Kai explained at Torri's expression. She removed her helmet from the shelf and tucked it under an arm then focused on Torri, apologetic and uncertain.

"I don't know what to say," she admitted.

"It's not your fault."

Kai ran her free hand through her hair and exhaled slowly. "I can't guarantee much right now because I don't know what's happening."

"And they're watching," Torri added. "That's not your fault, either." She regarded Kai, the Coalition uniform a tangible acknowledgement of the barrier that still divided them.

Kai walked past her to the outer room. Torri followed and waited as Kai stood near the door, seemingly studying the keypad. She turned. "I don't want to open this door," she said, voice brittle with emotion.

"I don't want you to, either." Torri kept her hands at her sides. Kai was on duty now and not approachable. She moved closer, waiting for Kai to do the inevitable, and for the door to slide open, sending them into another uncertain future.

"I'm not going to ask you what you're going to do or how you're planning to do it." Kai stared again at the keypad. "But you know enough to make whatever decisions you need to." She raised her gaze to Torri's for a split second before leaning in and kissing her, gentle but deep. "Until we meet again," she whispered as she pulled away. "Long life."

"And to you," Torri said, grief settling in her gut like cold rain.

Kai punched the code into the keypad, and the door slid open. "Go back the way we came in," she said. "They don't know about the back entrance. Four-four-six-eight." She hesitated and Torri waited, knowing she wanted to say something further. "If you ever—" She cleared her throat and moved her helmet to her other hand. "You can always reach me on the old frequency."

Torri stared at her, words frozen in her mouth. Kai turned away and scanned the corridor. Satisfied, she gestured with her head down the hallway toward the eatery. Torri joined her, and Kai closed and sealed the door. They regarded each other for a long moment, things unspoken clogging Torri's chest. Kai straightened into military persona. She nodded once, turned on her heel, and strode away from the door, away from the eatery. Torri watched her go, grappling with what had happened between them, and the fact that Kai had breached the boundary her uniform represented. She was wavering, Torri decided. The Coalition was losing its grip, but Kai realizing it and doing something about it were two very different things.

As if knowing what Torri was thinking—and Torri wouldn't doubt that such were possible—Kai shot a glance over her shoulder at her before she rounded a curve and disappeared. Torri headed back to the eatery, up the ramp, and to the metal door. She punched four-four-six-eight into the keypad, and the door opened. She entered, no one paying her any attention, and went back to the vendors' area beyond. The crowds hadn't decreased much, and Torri worked her way through into the gallery then back up the ramp to Newburg's surface. Two hours before Jindor arrived at the docks. She commed Saryl.

"Syl," came Saryl's voice in her skull.

"Problem."

"So it seems. Got word that security is tightening, and they're preparing for some kind of interrogations at fifteen hundred. Half the docks are empty, as everyone's left. Dal has us ready to leave, as well." Disappointment weighed in her voice.

Torri pulled her goggles out of her cargo pocket and adjusted them on her face. "Good. Prepare for a thirteen-thirty departure. Have Dal check the lander as well. I want everything in working order before we leave." She knew that Saryl would not miss the significance of her request with regard to the lander.

Saryl didn't respond for a moment but when she did, a trace of surprise colored her tone. "As you wish."

"Did you get a line on our former acquaintance's new colleague?"

"Miner at Vintooth. Coincidentally employed in the workshops."

*Coincidental indeed.* "Is he working today?"

"Funny you should ask. He goes on shift at eighteen hundred."

"How very convenient," Torri said. "And the other matter?"

Saryl paused, probably calling up information to send to Torri's wrist reader. "Biometrics match on the names."

Torri checked her reader. Jindor and Aylin were the same person, though Aylin had been declared dead on Shanlin three days after Torri's ship went down. At least that part of Jindor's past was true. "Well done." It couldn't have been easy to get that information. Saryl's data-tracking skills never ceased to amaze her.

"And are we still conducting a job interview?" Saryl asked.

"Absolutely. I'll be there in a half-hour."

"Excellent. Out."

Torri broke the connection and stopped at a vendor for hasha and a meat skewer, wishing that she was back in bed with Kai. She walked as she ate, thoughts sliding down Kai's naked body, like the sweat that collected between them and tasted of salt and sex. She caught herself, shaken, and finished the last piece of meat as the skewer dissolved. Torri stopped and drained the hasha container, the liquid racing down her throat with its customary jolt. Time to focus. She'd sort through her feelings about Kai later. The beverage container dissolved as well, and Torri wiped her hand on her pants as she approached the entrance to the loading docks.

The guards lounging around the security station were not Kai's contingent, from their informal demeanor. Torri approached the commanding officer, a human female, helmetless but wearing goggles. She stood stiffly near the queue that waited to enter the docking area. The line moved much slower today than in the past. That could be a problem for Jindor, since the guards seemed to be employing extra scrutiny to everyone.

"Lieutenant," Torri addressed the CO. "If I may interrupt?"

The other woman looked at her, suspicious but also

ill-at-ease. Her superiors hadn't given her many instructions, and she wasn't experienced enough to operate independently. That made her malleable but also twitchy. Torri smiled ingratiatingly. Always good to butter up the local CO. "I'm Syl t'Dorrin, trader from Endor Quadrant. We're interviewing a potential navigator at twelve hundred hours, and I wanted to ensure that I was following proper security procedure."

The lieutenant drew herself up a bit. "Name of interviewee?"

"Jindor Korickis. Shall I wait for her here?"

"I think that would be best. New security measures in place, after all."

Torri inclined her head. "My thanks for your time."

"When she gets here," the lieutenant said, "let me know."

"I will. Thank you." Torri offered a smile and moved away from the entrance, scanning the street. Still a half-hour before Jindor's arrival, but at least she'd be able to get a read on the general Newburg mood and maybe hear some gossip. She wandered closer to the queue, catching snatches of conversation. Quite a few talking about the Vintooth crack-down. Kai had been right. News always got out. Nobody knew much about what was happening, however. Two mentioned that the price of opals was going through the roof on the markets. Torri filed that tidbit away for later.

"Trader t'Dorrin," came Jindor's voice from behind her.

Torri turned. "Well met. Due to increased security, it was recommended that I wait for you here and accompany you to the ship." She appraised Jindor's clothing. Tan trousers, brown shirt, scuffed black boots. She carried a duffle bag.

"Many thanks."

Torri motioned her toward the CO she'd spoken with earlier. "Lieutenant, my party has arrived." She took her goggles off and stowed them in her pocket.

"IDs." The CO held out her hand, and both Torri and

Jindor provided their ID sticks. The lieutenant slid first one then the other into her wrist reader. Apparently seeing nothing untoward, she motioned them to step to the front of the line and personally lowered the force shield, much to the grumbling of those still waiting. Jindor shot a look at Torri, moderately surprised. "Friends in high places?" she asked as they entered the corridor.

"No. Just observant." Torri raised an eyebrow. "I take it you're aware of the situation at Vintooth."

"I am. And I've made the requisite adjustments."

Torri glanced at her as they walked. Jindor's features remained serene.

"I expect you have, as well." Jindor shifted the duffle bag to her other shoulder.

"Indeed." Torri maintained silence to the hangar, gauging Jindor's demeanor. Relaxed and casual. Which could be a good thing or a bad, depending on her loyalties. At the hangar entrance, a Coalition guard met them and demanded their IDs. Torri's he handed back. Jindor's he kept for a long moment before he turned his flat silver gaze to Torri.

"Business?"

"My crew and I are interviewing Korickis as a possible navigator. We filed a report a few days ago with regard to this matter. I had to let one of my crew go."

He removed Jindor's ID stick from his wrist reader and handed it back to her. "File another report if you hire her."

"Most assuredly. Thank you." Torri half-smiled and inclined her head. She didn't recognize him and decided not to push her luck. She motioned Jindor toward the ship, one of only five remaining in the bays. Saryl was right. The Coalition crackdown had sent most traders and merchants running. She had no doubt it was part of the market squeeze.

"Nice vessel," Jindor said appreciatively as they approached the boarding ramp. "Her name?"

"In good time. What do you see?" Torri triggered her commlink to both Saryl and Jann with a thought.

Jindor stopped at the ramp's foot, appraising the ship's sleek lines, exterior blackened and scored in places from travel. "Class two cargo vessel, TerraStar model. The position of the rear thrusters is common on pre-Coalition designs. This one is eight Earth years old, from the wing shape." She moved the duffle back to her left shoulder and approached the hull. "Forthin heat panels. She was constructed here on Earth but retro-fitted with updates elsewhere."

Jindor studied the metallic sheen of the underside, some six feet above her. "Vector Quadrant," she announced. "The primary updates were done there, as the underside panels are hexagonal, something the Coalition started using there on its cargo craft four years ago. The Magellan factories improved on the design, and that's what you've got here. Much better at withstanding warp jumps and atmospheric entries." She returned to the ramp.

"Well done," Torri said noncommittally.

"I'm not finished." Jindor leaned closer to Torri and lowered her voice. "She's been altered. You must have a hell of a crew because it's ingenious, really, what you've done. Pulsar and plasma cannon capability, masked in standard-issue and Coalition regulation laser sheaths. Plus, the thrusters have been re-tooled for fighter capacity."

"How so?" Torri crossed her arms and allowed the hint of a smile to play at the corners of her mouth.

"The cowling. Regulation on a TerraStar like this is one meter in diameter. Here, it's easily one and a sixth. Not enough to draw attention, but enough for class three fighter power and speed." Jindor regarded Torri. "You flew a class five at Shanlin, so a mid-grade three would be pretty easy for you to deal with. But it's tricky if you don't have at least a thousand hours in the air. Most Coalition squadrons these days are ones and twos, though their elites fly fours. The best Academy-trained flew fives." Jindor left that statement in the space between them, whether an opening or a warning Torri wasn't sure.

"I think I like her," Saryl announced from the top of the ramp, where she stood half-leaning out the door, arms braced above her head on the inside of the entrance.

"I rather thought you might," Torri said, not taking her eyes off Jindor's. She motioned toward the ramp. "Shall we?"

Something that could have been humor flashed across Jindor's face as she broke eye contact first and ascended the ramp, Torri a few paces behind. As Torri entered the ship, Saryl gave her a knowing look that passed as quickly as it came.

"Jindor Korickis, my second-in-command, Birrit Cansi. And—" Torri gestured toward Jann. "My chief engineer, Dal Greybern. Birrit will continue the interrogation," she said, smiling. "My thanks for putting yourself in the line of fire."

Jindor lowered her duffle to the grating underfoot. "I only do so if I trust the aim."

Saryl coughed into her closed fist, attempting to conceal a grin, and Jann suddenly found his boots extremely interesting. Torri picked up Jindor's bag. "Carry on, then. I'll just take up the rear," she said with mock imperiousness. And for the next forty-five minutes, she did just that as Saryl and Dal grilled Jindor on virtually every aspect of navigation, charting, ship specifications, and even political situations in the quadrants in which they did the most business. Jindor handled it well, Torri noted, watching her reactions. *Used to being in tight spots.* Able to make quick adjustments in her thinking and actions. Willing to learn from others. Torri liked Jindor's confidence, instilled through years of experience. *The difference between confidence and hubris is attitude*, came Instructor Stran's melodious voice. *Confidence in one's abilities comes from time, work, and a willingness to accept both defeat and victory and learn from both.*

Jindor fielded a question from Saryl about cargo specs, answering it in such a way that Torri knew she had done time on long- and short-haul freighters. *Hubris indicates an inability to learn the self. Those who engage in it overestimate their strengths and abilities. This makes them dangerous. But also predictable.*

Torri caught Saryl's eye, and Saryl nodded once and abruptly shifted the interview. "And now for the more active part of the hiring process," she said, throwing a glance at Jann, who acknowledged her with a smile. He retreated from the cargo bay. Torri moved aside in the narrow corridor as he passed, on his way to the bridge. Torri checked her wrist reader. Thirteen-twenty. Right on schedule.

Saryl activated the ship's jammers. "I trust you're aware of security changes at Vintooth Matrix?" she asked.

"Most definitely." Jindor's demeanor remained relaxed but alert.

"And I trust you're aware of the business we have there." Saryl voiced it as a statement.

"I am."

"Good. Because the second part of your interview starts now." Saryl nodded at Torri as she exited. "Captain. Prepare for departure." She turned the jammers off.

The ship's engines rumbled into life, and Torri caught Jindor's eye, assessing. Satisfied, she motioned with her head for Jindor to follow her to the bridge. Once there, she buckled into her customary seat at the controls and activated the jammers again. Saryl sat on Torri's right, and Jann took the far portside position. Cyr's seat, immediately to Torri's left, remained empty. "Plot us a convenient orbit," Torri instructed. "One that allows a lander ready access from Vintooth. Should a quick exit be in order." She kept the jammers on. They had ten minutes before port authority queried them about it.

Jindor lowered herself into Cyr's seat almost reverently and clipped the harness into place, adjusting it over her chest. Once settled, she looked at Torri, a question in her eyes.

"Key yourself," Torri said.

Jindor placed her right palm flat on the reader pad near Torri's left hand then, once the system calibrated itself to her, she brought up the screen of Austra Province, fingers flying over the controls. "I'm placing you here," she stated, a thin blue line snaking from the image of Earth to a point that triangulated with Newburg and Vintooth. "It's a common approach angle for the far matrices, and traders use it all the time to avoid the windstorms that come in with the jet stream. You have about a twenty-mile space eddy here—" she adjusted a reading and entered it into the system. "And you'll have a two-hour time window before security asks your business. Where are you headed after the pick-up?"

"Paltor Quadrant, via the Slipstream Trade Route."

Jindor's hands moved over the opaque surface of the control panel like she'd been born to it, like she'd designed the ship's interior herself. A little smile played at the right side of her mouth, and the green and blue glow from the screen cast a strange pallor over her face.

Torri turned the jammers off and made some adjustments to the underside hover thrusters before she opened a communication channel with the hangar. "Cargo Vessel Far Seek requesting departure clearance." She waited, knowing a security probe was wending its way through the ship's memory banks and conducting an interior scan.

"Declaration?" came a guttural male voice with an accent Torri couldn't place.

"Four crates of jewel-crafting tools, two calibrated for Slatelock Matrix, two for Vintooth."

"Destination?"

"Endor Quadrant, Farnessi Workshops."

Pause. "Ah. Trader Syl t'Dorrin. Awaiting voucher. One moment."

Torri checked the route Jindor had plotted. Efficient, and not one that would arouse suspicion.

"Voucher received."

Ten seconds stretched into thirty and thirty into sixty. Too long. Something wasn't right. Torri exchanged a wary glance with Saryl. Another thirty seconds passed. A new voice filled the bridge. Female, pleasant enough. If it weren't a monotone.

"Trader t'Dorrin, it is requested that you report to the hangar base immediately."

Jann swore softly, and Jindor's eyes widened.

"Certainly. Can I ask what this might be about?" Torri kept her tone pleasant as well, and cooperative. She'd had too many dealings with Coalition shills to press her luck here, though she ticked off possibilities in her head. Something Cyr had said? Had Kai's quarters been under surveillance? Ice filled Torri's veins. That was a possibility. *Oh, Cyllea, please don't let it be that.* Saryl's long fingers hovered over the ignition panel. Torri shook her head, and Saryl pulled her hand back.

"Standard security procedure," responded the female voice. "An escort has been dispatched."

"Very well. And my crew?"

"It would be most helpful if they remained with your ship."

"Of course. Out." Torri closed the commline and unbuckled her harness. "Stand down," she directed as she pushed herself out of her seat. She held Saryl's gaze. "Eighteen hundred. Complete the contract." *As best you can*, she finished silently.

Saryl's jaw muscles clenched, and for a moment, Torri thought she might refuse an order from her. "Eighteen hundred," Saryl repeated softly. To Jindor she said, "Plot us to Endor Quadrant."

Torri left the bridge, Jann at her heels. She lowered the ramp to the hangar floor. Two armed and helmeted Coalition guards stood waiting for her. One female, one male, by body shape.

An escort like this for one trader. Did they know who she was? Or was this about her night with Kai? She would claim that she had picked Kai up in a bar. Sexual trysts were something people understood in a place like Newburg. Torri continued studying the guards, but their body language didn't tell her much beyond the fact that they didn't seem to know much about her or this situation. Which played in Torri's favor.

"We're not leaving without you," Jann said behind her and near her shoulder. Without turning, Torri gauged him near the door panel.

"Eighteen hundred," Torri said again, not looking at him. Saryl would take care of the contract. She'd find a way out of Newburg even without Torri at the Far Seek's helm. And Saryl could get them underground again and build a business with their current clients, if this "security matter" ended in a worst-case scenario. Torri thought then of Kai, and a flash of regret left a pain in her chest. "We all come to the end of our paths," she said. "Don't cut yours short if I've reached mine." She walked down the ramp before he could say anything more.

## CHAPTER 10

"Officers," she said politely as she approached. They carried pistols in their holsters, but only the male looked like he actually had practice with it. The female kept fiddling with the butt of hers, indicating that the holster was new to her belt. Or at least uncommon. Something about her was familiar. Torri glanced at the ID strip on the guard's left pectoral. Ah. Of course. The lieutenant with whom she'd cleared Jindor.

"Trader Syl t'Dorrin," the lieutenant stated in formal Coalition. Not a question. She recognized Torri.

Torri nodded. "Lieutenant. My thanks for serving as one of my escorts," she responded in Coalition, maintaining a relaxed formality, acknowledging that she, too, was aware that they had already met.

"Please come with us." The lieutenant turned on her heel, and Torri fell into step behind her, the other guard taking a position behind her. They walked in silence out of the hangar into a long corridor tiled with flat pale yellow stones from floor to roof, glow tubes in the ceiling creating a harsher ambiance here than probably warranted. The soles of their boots scuffed on the floor, the sound bouncing off the walls, strangely distorted.

Torri studied the female guard's form, noting her carriage. Serious about her duties, but slightly tentative. Perhaps recently promoted. Also young. The Coalition often promoted soldiers as favors to wealthy or well-placed families. There was, thus, a possibility that the lieutenant was the daughter of a prominent Coalition official or political ally who wasn't quite up to the position but knew she had to take it or risk some kind of political fall-out. The Coalition liked to appear magnanimous in things like military promotions, but in reality, such served two purposes. To bind allies closer and to extend control. Nobody ever declined a Coalition promotion. Doing so incurred risk to livelihood and, often, life.

They turned left, and the floor sloped down as they proceeded another hundred yards before the lieutenant stopped at a door. She pressed her bare thumb to the keypad and it slid open. She motioned for Torri to go in.

"Someone will be with you in a bit," she said as Torri entered.

The door slid shut behind Torri, and she waited a few seconds, calming herself, preparing. She remained standing by the door, studying her surroundings. Standard interrogation room. Maybe ten feet square. A rectangular table about two feet wide and three feet long stood in the center of the room, one chair on each of the long sides. Neither of the chairs faced the door. No windows, no visible scanners. Smooth white walls and more harsh lighting. Designed for discomfort.

Torri fiddled with her wrist reader, like someone who was nervous might. She triggered its recording capabilities, though to an observer, it appeared to be powered off. She meandered around the small confines, maintaining the illusion that she was merely waiting to get this over with so she could be on her way. They were watching, she knew. Gauging her body language. Recording her pulse rate and cross-referencing her biometrics.

Torri wasn't worried about that. She had chosen this identity carefully, going through hundreds of possibilities before finding Syl t'Dorrin and resurrecting her from an obscure database affiliated with an even more obscure trader genealogy once rooted in the soils of what might have been Greece or

Turkey. The main trunk of the family tree died three hundred years before Torri's birth, and the various branches had long since intertwined with other lines until the t'Dorrin genes were no longer a distinct track to any specific ancestor.

Syl's profile proved a good physiological and ethnic match for Torri, and her given name appeared throughout the t'Dorrin lineage. A family name. One that was common, and made its way into the other lines that absorbed the last of the t'Dorrins. Torri's namesake had died before she turned thirty-five, in the Fortunata Wars before the ascendance of the Empire. There hadn't been enough of her to salvage for cell storage, another reason Torri chose her. No one could definitively prove Torri wasn't a t'Dorrin, which always played in her favor.

The door slid open behind her, and she turned. An Earthman entered, wearing the maroon robe of a local Coalition official. It stretched tight over his paunch. How strange, Torri found herself thinking, that he would allow such a thing to happen to his body. He stood regarding her with eyes the color of sapphires. Unblinking. Unfeeling. Half-syn, probably. He was bald, and his skull reminded Torri of a milky opal in shape and color.

"Trader t'Dorrin," he said in standard Coalition with the accent of Austra Province. "Please, sit."

Torri considered his offer. No doubt the chair he indicated served other purposes than merely sitting. "Many thanks, Regent, but I much prefer standing. Long flights make one restless. Will you forgive this rather odd quirk of mine?" She clasped her hands behind her back, affecting an apologetic air. His syn self would register it as nothing more than something that happened. But the human part of his brain might take umbrage. She risked it.

He blinked, and in the motion his eyes shifted to brown, like a solar shield descending over a porthole. More than half-syn. "Very well," he said as he took the chair that put the table between them.

He placed a porta-reader on the table's surface and focused on its monitor. "Syl t'Dorrin, Endor Quadrant. Though you were born here on Earth."

Torri said nothing. This, too, was standard interrogation procedure. He would reveal how much they knew, some of which was deliberately false, fishing for more information.

He glanced at her then back at the reader. "Trader with merchant status. Many clients throughout Endor and a few in Paltor. When was the last time you were in Hallifin?"

"A year, maybe a bit more," she answered smoothly, unruffled at his attempt to unsettle her with the abrupt shift. Not a lie. Not quite the truth.

"Your business in Newburg?"

"Gem tools. I'm contracted with the Farnessi workshops, Endor branch."

His pudgy fingers worked the reader panel. "Slatelock Matrix. And Vintooth." He looked up at her. "The tools Farnessi requested are calibrated for both." It was not a question.

Torri inclined her head in acknowledgment. "Fire opals, mostly, from Slatelock. Pure-color black from Vintooth, though it's the fire that are popular in Endor at the moment. Especially the amber and rust colors. Would the Regent like to view the shipment?" she asked, the obsequious phrasing that standard Coalition incorporated grating across her nerves though she didn't let it show.

He ignored the question. "Jindor Korickis," he said instead. "You're acquainted with her."

"I am. She is, in fact, on my ship."

He pursed his lips, watching the reader. "For an interview. And have you decided whether she will become part of your crew?"

"I have not. I was hoping to do so as soon as possible, but my presence was required here." Interrogation games. She, too, fished for information, revealing some things but not others, seeing where her responses would take the questions.

"Rozin Hester."

Torri waited.

"Korickis would replace Hester," he elaborated after a moment.

"If I believe her an appropriate and capable replacement, yes." Torri shifted forward slightly, rocking onto the balls of her feet then back to her heels, a show of restlessness for surveillance that was no doubt occurring outside the room.

"Majan." He looked up at her, irises shifting back to blue. A crucial question. One she had to answer correctly.

"Regent?" Torri pretended polite confusion.

"Pure-color stones," he said, changing his approach. His eyes shifted color again. "What is their current market value?"

"It depends on their matrices of origin, their cut, and the workshop. A Slatelock pure-color brings forty thousand through retailers. But a Vintooth brings a hundred thousand."

"Two hundred thousand," he corrected. "There seems to be a shortage of Vintooth pure-colors this week."

She inclined her head. "A pity, then, that I'm not running stones this trip," she said, tone betraying nothing.

He made no response and focused again on the reader.

"Your crew filed for a thirteen-thirty departure. You've completed your business here?"

"With the exception of a full hire for Korickis, yes."

"Your shipping permits don't mention stones," he said, and in his tone Torri heard a trap. "What will I find if I search your ship?"

"Gem tools calibrated for Slatelock and Vintooth. And one synthetic pure-color opal."

He looked up at her, and the alabaster sheen of his skin reflected the light. Not much human left of him, Torri decided.

"Synthetic?"

"A good one," she said with a slight smile that she knew he wouldn't register.

"Just one?"

She shrugged, a "that's how things worked out" motion. "Cards. Had I known it was a synthetic, I wouldn't have let the other player off so easy."

He regarded her for a long moment, expressionless. Like a machine. The door slid open, and the lieutenant who had accompanied Torri from her ship stood on the threshold, her faceplate up. Torri estimated her to be in her early twenties. She read her name and rank on the small metal strip over her left pectoral.

"Regent?" the lieutenant addressed him.

"Please accompany Trader t'Dorrin to Major Rila."

The lieutenant half-bowed from the waist and stepped toward Torri, hand on the butt of her gun. Torri hooked her hands on her belt where the guard could see them and waited, expectant. The lieutenant gestured at the corridor with her chin, and Torri preceded her out of the interrogation room. The male guard was gone. The Regent had most likely dismissed him, probably assuming that Torri wouldn't make a break for it this deep in Coalition territory.

They were headed farther away from the hangar, toward the mines. Torri felt rather than heard the deep thrum of mechanical devices, drilling and ripping their way deeper into the veins of the earth, bleeding the soil of opals and transfusing greed into petty local officials. She sensed the lieutenant's nervousness. Not necessarily a rookie, but definitely her first security detail. If local Coalition officials had known who Torri really was, they would have put a more experienced contingent on her. She relaxed a bit, keeping her hands hooked on her belt. They passed a few more Coalition soldiers, all wearing weapons, though no one seemed in any kind of hurry.

Ten minutes later, the corridor snaked to the right. Here, the sound of mining machinery was louder, a low hum that seemed to vibrate within the walls. More soldiers and a few people

Torri figured were somehow affiliated with the mines passed them, a few glancing at her curiously. Special clearance, no doubt, to be in this particular corridor.

"Lieutenant Fandiz," Torri said in Coalition without stopping or turning around. "May I trouble you a bit? Might I ask who Major Rila is?"

"She's responsible for Newburg security," came the brusque reply.

*Most likely a career soldier, then.* Torri waited a beat before speaking again. "My apologies, Lieutenant, but I have no idea why I'm here. Is there some problem with my ship's voucher?"

"I wouldn't know," Fandiz said in clipped tones. "I'm a security escort."

*Nothing more, nothing less*, Torri finished silently. She waited another beat. "Regardless, my thanks for your direction earlier today. I greatly appreciate it."

Fandiz didn't reply this time. Torri continued walking in silence for a few more minutes.

"Here," Fandiz said, stopping at another nondescript door. She thumbed the keypad, and it opened onto a scene that reminded Torri of her Academy days, when she and her classmates were preparing to go on a training mission in the common areas of the barracks. Small groups of soldiers stood around talking while others were engaged in studying wall readers. A holoscreen projected the entire province, topographic features in thin green and blue lines, other features—including settlements and mines—designated in other colors. Three soldiers monitored it. The opposite wall was glass, floor to ceiling, and looked out across a vast lighted cavern. Torri caught glimpses of mining equipment through the dust that hung like clouds near the cavern's ceiling. The vibration in her legs tickled.

A senior officer approached. Not a captain, but a bar over a lieutenant. He easily had six inches on Saryl. "Lieutenant?" He addressed Fandiz.

"Regent Gib requested an audience with Major Rila for Trader t'Dorrin." She toyed nervously with the butt of her gun.

He turned his flat silver gaze to Torri. "Very well. Wait here." He turned on his heel, an abrupt but smooth motion, and went to the opposite side of the room where he addressed a much shorter figure.

Fandiz shifted her weight from foot to foot. Clearly she hadn't had much experience dealing with these sorts of situations, further evidence that she was new to her rank. Torri's own recalcitrance about accepting anyone's rank as something to be automatically respected flared, and she fought an urge to tell the private that it was all for show, that a title meant nothing. *We're all naked underneath our clothes.*

The officer returned. Career soldier, partially syn, from his eyes. But human enough that he was proud of his work. "Major Rila will speak with you." He glanced past Torri's shoulder at Fandiz. "Dismissed."

Torri turned her head and caught the Fandiz's gaze. "My thanks for your professionalism."

Fandiz started, surprised. She nodded once and straightened, holding her chin a little higher.

"Trader," the male officer repeated.

Torri followed him to whom she surmised was Major Rila, a short, wiry figure dressed in Coalition grey, her rank visible in three crimson stripes on her left arm. She stood looking out over the mine, hands clasped behind her back, hair so black it was almost blue.

"Major, Trader t'Dorrin," the officer said in Coalition. He clicked his heels and bowed slightly from the waist.

She turned from the window, and Torri dipped her head in civilian recognition of a high-ranking military official. "Major

Rila," Torri said in acknowledgment, also addressing her in Coalition. "How may I be of service?" She took a chance, and from the gaze Rila affixed to her, her approach was the right one.

"Syl t'Dorrin," Rila said, pronouncing the name with a thoughtful, detached air. She looked up at the male officer. "Dismissed."

He saluted, right fist on left pectoral, and retreated. The major returned her attention to Torri, who stood a couple inches taller. But Major Rila was a woman used to getting what she wanted, no matter her physical build, and the aura she exuded assured Torri that she had no qualms doing something herself if necessary. She bore the demeanor of a professional warrior, confident but quiet. She'd seen things, probably done worse, and bore the weight of decisions both right and wrong, not losing much sleep over either. In this woman Torri saw Kai, if Kai stayed with the Coalition. The thought bothered her.

"I have need of a trader whose discretion comes highly recommended," the major said, meeting Torri's gaze with her dark eyes. No boundaries existed between her pupils and irises, which merged into ebony circles. Pronounced, sharp-edged cheekbones, two thin scars beneath the left. Radij heritage. *Interesting.* And mixed-blood, most likely, or she wouldn't have been able to leave her homelands.

"I would assume that the recommendation is one the major gives some weight to." Torri's thumbs remained hooked on her belt, and she exuded impassivity at this turn of events.

A flicker of curiosity—or was it amusement?—crossed the major's face. "In a manner of speaking." She turned and looked again through the window. "Have you had the opportunity to visit the mines during your visit?"

"No, I'm afraid I have not been so fortunate." Torri followed Rila's lead and looked out the window as well, at the massive drilling rigs anchored to shaft entrances, bracing legs splayed, arachnid-like, over the openings. Miners wearing brainjacks manned each rig, guiding the equipment's sentient intelligence deeper into the rock of Austra Province. That's why some miners went a little dodgy after a few years. Jacking the rigs too long took a toll on body *and* mind. Torri watched a crew maneuver a new rig into place against an unmarred wall. Like a spider, it gripped the stone with its limbs and placed its bit against the hard surface, its handler guiding it through whatever topographic image he had floating in his brain through the jackprobe.

"Then your luck is changing," The major said, not turning her head. "Please accompany me on a tour."

It was not a request, and Torri didn't reply. Instead, she followed the major out another door into yet another corridor that looked a lot like the first though not as wide. The major didn't speak as they walked, ignoring the soldiers who stopped in their tracks and snapped to attention as she approached. Torri didn't try to make conversation. The major was not the kind of woman who would engage in small talk for no reason other than passing the time. She outranked everyone they passed, an indication that Fandiz was right, and that Rila was most likely one of the top Coalition military officials at the Newburg mines. Maybe in Newburg.

Had Majan passed her name to Rila? Torri ran through possibilities. For what purpose? That made little sense. Majan had as much riding on this contract as Torri did. Then again, the Coalition may have paid her more than the contract was worth. Torri let her hands swing free of her belt. She flexed her fingers. But chances were, Majan's client was also Coalition. Had Majan gotten caught in Coalition cross-fire? Maybe the Coalition wanted Majan's client. They'd figured out he was trying to corner the market. Then again, so many Coalition officials were corrupt that chances were, they'd want a piece of the contract.

This had the makings of a supreme double-cross, and Torri had to play her hand very, very carefully. The corridor ended at a metal double door some ten feet square, a jagged line five feet from the floor delineating how the two halves fit together. Two soldiers stood on either side, those on the right at a porta-reader, probably cross-checking biometrics. When they saw the major, they all straightened to attention.

"At ease," she said, and one triggered the door. It opened like a mouth to a loading dock and a dull roaring and pounding. A blast of moist heat emanated from the mine, like breath from a subterranean monster. Torri smelled dirt and the pungent tang of heavy machinery. The major walked through, not checking to see if Torri followed. The guards didn't even look at her as she did.

They went right, to a covered floater parked in one of the slots. Another soldier saluted then stepped forward and opened the floater's hatch. The major climbed into the driver's seat, and Torri took the passenger seat on her right. She buckled the harness as the major did the same before she closed the hatch. A few seconds later, the major engaged the thrusters and backed the craft out of its slot. She steered it to what might have been a shaft and accelerated into its black confines. Not a shaft. A transport corridor. Blue light strips in the ceiling flickered and flashed past like stars at warp jump. The shaft's walls were barely a foot from either side of the floater, but the major guided it with one hand on the controls, relaxed. Focused.

Torri considered her options. She wasn't dead or imprisoned yet, which gave her a little maneuverability. Someone had put Rila in touch with her, and whatever this was about, it wasn't standard Coalition politics. If Torri did whatever Rila was going to propose, it would probably put her in a world of hurt with the Coalition and with the client she was supposed to make the drop to in a couple of weeks. If she didn't, she had no doubt that Rila would make sure nothing much was left of her, if anything. *Beware of factions within a political front. Always find the starting point of each thread and see where it leads.* Torri triggered the commlink in her ear and sent a ping to Saryl, though as far down as they were, she might not get it.

"Rozin Hester," Major Rila said in the same thoughtful tone she'd used earlier.

Cyr. He *had* gone to the Coalition. So the miner he'd contacted was a Coalition informant? But why would Cyr go directly to the Coalition? He'd want a cut of the action, and the Coalition wouldn't give him anything beyond a patronizing thank you for doing his "duty" in uncovering black market schemes. Torri waited for Rila to continue.

"A man with a grudge."

"A man with a problem," Torri responded, "and not enough funds to support it." She didn't use the major's title. It would have sounded contrived, and Rila, she knew, had already attuned herself to a few aspects of Torri's personality. This was a matter that was underground, both literally and figuratively, and no title had any meaning beyond a context for recognition.

"A man like that could be dangerous to former employers."

"A man like that is dangerous regardless."

Rila made a noise in her throat that might have been an affirmative. Or it might not have meant anything at all. "The market for Vintooth pure-color, as I'm sure you're aware," she said in a bored tone, "has made it quite profitable to sell. Provided, of course, one has such a product."

"Or perhaps the means to secure such a product." Torri played one of her cards, testing Rila's hand.

The major didn't respond right away, and Torri said nothing further. After a few minutes, Rila spoke again. "I'm under the impression that you're well aware of the Vintooth markets."

That was all Cyr knew before Torri had relieved him of his position. So he'd contacted a Coalition informant and that informant contacted Rila. The question now was what specifically Rila wanted. "In my line of work, it's something I follow, yes." Torri kept her tone conversational. Coalition didn't offer the nuances that Empire did in its linguistic infrastructure, making it harder to tease out subtexts. She thus chose her words carefully.

"There's a rumor about a possible theft of a shipment of Vintooth pure-colors," Rila said, almost conversational.

"And also a rumor about increased security at Vintooth. As it should be, to prevent such occurrences."

The major adjusted the floater's speed and relaxed into her seat as the craft noticeably slowed. Cruising speed. "Or prevent any pure-color from that matrix from reaching legitimate markets." She had switched to Empire, and the almost musical tones of her Radij accent added extra layers to an already richly textured language. Compared to Coalition, Empire was an explosion of aural color.

"If that were a concern." Torri's inflection on the last part of her response indicated that she knew a market squeeze was on, but she wasn't placing blame anywhere.

"We understand each other, then," Rila said, still using Empire.

Yes, Torri understood only too well. Rila was on the take somehow, and Torri was the catalyst. She doubted Cyr knew that when he made contact with the informant. And now Cyr, too, was about to get screwed. Rila might toss the informant a bone, but Cyr could rot in a Newburg alley for all she'd care.

"Markets are difficult to gauge," Torri said, adding a note of uncertainty to her phrasing. "Anything might cause instability." And if Torri failed in whatever Rila had planned, Rila wasn't out anything but Torri could either end up doing time on a Coalition penal colony or dead. Not attractive options. But If Torri succeeded so, too, did Rila. A more attractive option, but one that still rankled. *I'm no better than a fucking Coalition shill.* The thought stuck in her throat like bad liquor.

"True." The major slowed the vehicle even more, guiding it down a right-hand shaft that joined the main at an angle. Torri heard the crackling of a force shield as it dissolved. The major must have triggered a code inside the floater. She stopped about fifty yards in, and only the soft glow from the control panel alleviated the darkness outside the floater. "One missing shipment might cause quite a bit of instability, in a market already in fluctuation. Hard to say what two missing shipments could cause." Rila raised the hatch, and cooler air washed over Torri, bearing damp undercurrents.

Rila unbuckled her harness and lowered the floater closer to what Torri guessed was the ground. She flicked on the vehicle's exterior lights, climbed out, and busied herself with what Torri presumed was a portside storage compartment. The floater's lights afforded her a glimpse of this tunnel. Maybe six feet up, six feet across, pockmarked basalt walls. She unbuckled her harness. Her trip with Rila no doubt ended here. The major finished what she was doing and went around the back of the floater to stand on the starboard side as Torri exited the craft. She held a pack about twelve inches square in her left hand and in her right a porta-light. She handed that to Torri.

"There's a lot one might do, with an extra shipment of Vintooth pure-colors," Rila said. Her eyes were indistinguishable from the darkness that lay beyond the floater's circle of light. "Provided one was able to procure it." She held up the pack, and Torri took it. Maybe a pound. Without another word the major returned to the driver's side of the floater and got in. She buckled up, closed the hatch, and reversed out of the corridor, dragging what light the craft provided with her. The force shield engaged with a muted snap.

Torri listened for the sound of the floater's thrusters engaging in the main tunnel—a click, hum, and whine that dissipated in seconds. She waited in the dark, acclimating herself to this environment. A soft wooshing from the main corridor. Distant, hollow thumping. And air that blew over her face, pulled from somewhere to somewhere else. She turned the light on and set the pack on the floor so she could inspect its contents.

A wrist reader, a military canteen—probably military-issue go juice—and a pistol in a holster. Two ammo cylinders. That was pretty good firepower. Maybe a thousand rounds. Overkill? Or was there something else the major wanted her to know? Torri removed the wrist reader and examined it with her porta-light. Rila wouldn't risk something trackable like this. She turned it over and saw the microcomm on the underside of the face, stuck there using a light-sensitive adhesive. She trained the porta-light on it, and five seconds later it fell from the reader into her palm.

Torri activated her own wrist reader's scanning capabilities. It blinked an affirmative when it calibrated to the microcomm and captured its information. Once done, the disk dissolved in her hand. She put the other wrist reader into one of her cargo pockets and removed the blaster from the pack. Standard-issue small arm, something every Coalition soldier carried. She turned it on, and it started humming, running a system check. Its read-out told her it was already fully loaded. Fifteen hundred rounds total. Torri straightened and attached the holster to her belt, right side, butt facing forward. She preferred a cross-body draw, and this position also made it difficult for someone behind her to remove it. She placed the ammo cylinders in her left-hand front pocket, where she could reach them quickly if necessary.

It had been a while since she'd been armed, but her body accepted the addition like an old friend come calling. Torri adjusted the pack to her body, wearing it near her lumbar region rather than across her shoulders, and joined the magnetic points of the straps. It nestled against her, conforming to her back, and she checked her reader, which displayed the map it had acquired from Rila's microcomm.

No doubt the pack harbored a tracker as well, and it was probably sending a signal to Rila's informant at Vintooth. Torri stood, assessing her surroundings and gathering her thoughts. Rila knew Torri was contracted for a contraband shipment of opals. Cyr seemed the most likely candidate as the source of that information, but Torri needed to think further about that. It made sense that he would be. Perhaps he contracted with the informant, who had promised him some of the take. What Cyr probably wasn't counting on was that he stood to gain nothing in this venture. Rila and her informant were using him. And they were using her, as well. She checked the map on her wrist reader again.

The corridor in which she was standing would take her to the southeastern edge of Vintooth Matrix, three miles away. Then another shaft that didn't appear in the data Saryl had tracked down would bring her to another tunnel that led to the matrix's main entrance. Saryl's investigation indicated that the workshops and holding gallery were located in the first cavern, a tenth of a mile from the entrance.

She checked her position. A half-mile underground. Saryl might get a ping. She sent another then attached the portalight to her shirt, angling the thin beam so it pointed in front of her. The light would pick up her body heat and stay charged. She stood a moment longer, clearing her mind of clutter. *In heightened states of awareness, focus can be easy to achieve but difficult to maintain. The mind can only withstand so much stress before wandering.*

Torri took several deep breaths through her mouth, exhaling through her nose, remembering how Instructor Harwood demonstrated various relaxation techniques. *You can extend your mind's ability to focus longer in situations of duress. Develop a place within it where there is one thing—and one thing only—to draw your attention. Use this focal point to ground yourself.*

She closed her eyes and went to her calming place, to the image that always infused her with peace, even in the worst situations. An image that had cemented itself in her mind a year before she took Instructor Harwood's course. Kai, walking on the tarmac outside the Academy hangar, dressed in her Cadet flight suit, carrying her helmet under her right arm. She'd just completed her first solo, four months before anyone else, with a perfect score, something only one other Cadet in Academy history had done. And as Kai approached Torri, a blazing winter sun her backdrop, she had grinned, an expression both jubilant and shy flickering on her features. She set her helmet on the floor and pulled Torri into a hug once she was close enough. The first time Kai had ever hugged her, three years into their Cadet training. Safe, warm, trusted. That's what Torri felt in that embrace, and that memory served as her focal anchor. She took a few more deep breaths, opened her eyes, and started walking.

## CHAPTER II

This shaft hadn't been in use for a while. Nearly two miles in, and Torri had seen no evidence of recent activity. Moisture slickened the floor in places and in others, softer veins of rock had crumbled, creating little piles that collected where the walls and floor met. She had taken the light off her shirt and clipped it to the left side of her belt instead, thus minimizing its motion.

Rila's plan was ingenious, really. She was on the take but needed someone who wasn't traceable, no matter what happened. And Rila had arranged this in such a way that Torri had limited options. If she said no, Rila could imprison her indefinitely for investigation. Or do something to her ship and crew. Torri gritted her teeth at that thought. So was it, in fact, Cyr who had alerted alerted Rila to Torri's "reputation"? Or was it someone else? Jindor?

Torri considered that but it didn't make sense because it put Jindor in a position with few options. And Jindor was careful about covering her ass. Back to Majan. It still didn't make sense, because Majan, too, stood to lose a lot if a high-ranking Coalition military official wanted some of the illicit stones trade. It was possible, however, that someone had put pressure on Majan, and the Miridian had felt forced to take a Coalition buy-out. Possible, but not necessarily probable. Hundreds of opal vendors and traders clogged Newburg, most of whom were no doubt dabbling in the black market. If Majan had talked, it was because the Coalition had specific information. And that could only have come from Jindor. Why would Jindor go Coalition? Torri mulled that for a moment.

The Coalition always appreciated finding a rebel who'd survived the Collapse to serve as examples of what could happen to those who plotted uprisings. But Torri hadn't been active in like-mind circles since Shanlin. She'd gone completely underground and concentrated instead on making a living, whether off illicit deals or not. She couldn't be linked to any active like-mind plots because she had "died" seven years ago. Unless Jindor had decided to create a link and plant it. But why?

Torri stopped to check the map on her wrist reader. She'd arrived at a third offshoot tunnel. It appeared on the map. Good. She kept moving, thinking. *Politics knows no friends. When following threads of intrigue to their source, one must consider every possibility.* Torri's stomach jerked, and she tasted bile. *Every possibility.* Kai? Would Kai put her in a position like this? She needed money to try to buy the Coalition off and keep them from converting her family's holdings. And Kai was desperately loyal to her family. Why, Torri didn't understand, given some of the things Kai had dealt with as a child. Kai on the take? All she had to do was ask, and Torri would get the money for her.

But Kai had been more effusive with her affections on this past meeting. Had she merely been lulling Torri into some kind of sense of security? Would Kai do that? The thought physically sickened her, and she stopped, bending over until the wave of nausea passed. She spat revulsion onto the corridor's floor. How could she think that of Kai? Her assigned bunkmate at the Academy? The person she'd come to trust with her life? She started walking again, trying to dispel her unease. *Every possibility.* She gritted her teeth and went back to her original list of suspects.

Cyr. That made the most sense. He'd been selling information to the Coalition. Kai had told her that. But maybe Kai wanted her to think that. *No. Cyr had been doing something with the Coalition.* He was slagged at Torri, and his addiction twisted his thinking. Even though he didn't know for sure who Torri's client was, the information might have been enough to get Rila's attention. Perhaps she even knew which official was creating the squeeze, and she was engaged in a little blackmail. Two shipments, she'd said. She knew Torri wanted one. But she wanted one, as well. If Torri didn't acquire it, she'd instead acquire an enemy with a lot of Coalition pull.

She thought again of Jindor. It was always possible to get fucked in more ways than just the pleasurable. Torri could have gotten careless. But it made little sense for Jindor to use Torri's past against her. Majan had run the check on her, after all. And found pretty much nothing beyond Trader. Jindor would've had to do a lot of work to create a recent past that would link Torri to a like-mind uprising or network. What would Jindor gain from that? The Coalition knew rebels had survived the Collapse. But unless those rebels remained actively plotting and engaged in revolution, the Coalition didn't waste too much energy on tracking them all down.

Realistically, Torri simply wasn't valuable to the Coalition because she hadn't been engaged in active rebellion since the Collapse. Still, her connections during that time and before might be useful if the Coalition was intelligence gathering. Still, trying to pin her for that seemed like too much effort for too little gain. And somehow, that didn't seem like Jindor's style.

She passed another offshoot tunnel, its entrance maybe three feet in diameter. The map on her reader registered three offshoots total. Which meant that the map was inaccurate or some of the tunnels were put in after the map had been created. That didn't make much sense, since mining companies were always sending recon probes into the shafts to check stability and activity. She came to a fifth offshoot, on the left, again about three feet in diameter and round. Curious, she stopped and examined its edges. Irregular and rough. This one had been blasted or lasered out. She took the light off her belt and shone it inside. It curved almost immediately to the right, a cramped snake hole of a tunnel. Fine grey dust had collected on the floor, probably leftovers from carving it.

She shone the light around, studying the offshoot's floor. Something had been coming and going here because a path of sorts had been scuffed into the dust. At least three sets of tracks left evidence of their passage in the thicker dust closer to the walls. Bipeds, though that didn't necessarily make Torri feel better about what the tracks might represent. One set was made by a pair of large boots, one she couldn't tell, and the other— she trained the light on it, trying to discern its edges without entering the offshoot. Bare feet. She licked an index finger and held it up, inside the smaller tunnel. It led somewhere, because she felt a breeze. Warm. She leaned in, sniffing. Something faint and fetid, like an animal burrow. And definitely not something she cared to learn more about. She shone the light behind her, back down the main shaft. Something moved. A lesser shadow, retreating beyond the beam.

Torri increased the power on the light to its maximum output, giving her another five feet. A thirty-foot range, now. She stood, listening and watching, cold sweat erupting on her back. A noise, out of place. The brush of something on stone, something that wasn't retreating. Torri switched the light to her right hand, and with her left pulled the pistol from its holster. She activated it with her thumb. *Never engage something you haven't identified and never invite engagement unless it is the best option for survival.* But no sense being unprepared, should something invite *her* to engage. She hadn't shot a pistol in three years, but in these confines accuracy and distance weren't an issue.

So here was a dilemma. The thing was behind her, which meant she might have to consider walking backward, so she could employ her light. Where there was one there had to be others, and if that was the case, they could be between her and Vintooth. *Cyllea, if I ever needed some guidance, now would be a good time.*

Torri backed away from the offshoot. Maybe whatever it was lived in there and it was just politely waiting for her to move away. She hugged the left-hand wall, walking in an awkward position, since she kept her right arm positioned so that the light shone behind her, which meant not much shone in front, but close to the wall like this, she didn't feel as exposed. It would be harder for whatever it was to launch itself at her if it risked careening into the wall. In the middle of the corridor, Torri was an easier target.

Fifty paces past the fifth offshoot she heard a scuffling from behind and a low grunt. Torri stopped, training the light in the direction of the offshoot. The beam didn't reach the opening, but something was definitely lingering just outside its perimeter.

"From the surface," came a low, guttural voice, speaking a variant of Empire Torri hadn't heard since she was a child. Her guts knotted, and adrenaline shot through her limbs. This was worse than some kind of non-human predator because animals were predictable. Humans or variants thereof were infinitely more dangerous.

The voice spoke again, this time just beyond the beam's reach. "Surface."

Torri jerked the light toward it and caught a pale, twisted figure that crouched on the corridor's floor. Human. Sort of. His hair was the color of the dust in the offshoot tunnel, long and matted, and it merged with his equally long and matted beard and moustache. He winced and closed his eyes before scooting back a few feet, out of the light. He wore black trousers, no shirt, and no shoes. Maybe someone who'd incurred the wrath of Rila? No, because the version of Empire he spoke indicated he'd been down here a long time. Some miner who got lost? Maybe. Maybe one who'd brainjacked too much with a drill rig.

"From the surface," he said in his harsh toneless monotone. "From the light." The Empire inflection he put on "light" indicated wonder and fear.

Torri continued walking, away from whoever the marooned man was. He'd been down here this long, he'd remain. Her heartbeat slowed as her initial shock at seeing him dissipated.

"Surface." A different voice.

Torri stopped and shone the light again back down the corridor. The first speaker stood just beyond its reach. A second stood to his left. Another human male, pale and gnarled like his companion, but bald. He looked like an alabaster statue, every rib visible, every corded muscle in his skinny arms and legs clearly defined. What was left of his pants barely covered his genitalia. He blinked in the light and turned his head away from it.

"Surface," the first echoed.

Torri licked her lips. The only option she had was to go on to Vintooth. Choosing again not to engage, she backed away, to see what they'd do. She took five steps, and they followed, just beyond the beam of her light. So far, they didn't seem interested in causing trouble. But that could change. She again hugged the wall and continued toward Vintooth, listening to the soft movements of her followers. She divided her attention between them and what might be in front, but she kept the light shining behind her.

A few more minutes passed, her right arm cramping in the position she held it. The men behind her hadn't spoken again but she knew they still followed. How much longer to Vintooth? She tried to check her wrist reader while she moved, but couldn't make out the map on the small screen. She'd have to stop to do so, and that might not be a good idea. She bit back a curse. This day was not shaping up to her liking.

*And it just got even worse.* She stopped, listening. Another visitor, this one between her and Vintooth. Not the best position to be in. One decent light, potential attack from two directions. She activated the laser pointer on her pistol and shone it down the tunnel toward Vintooth, keeping her porta-light trained on the two behind her. The pistol sight glanced off another pale form. She heard scrabbling from up ahead and moved the sight from one side of the corridor to the other. At least two more, plus the two behind her. She turned to check on them and bit back an oath. Five total, now.

Torri positioned her back against the wall, right hand pointed the way she had come, holding the porta-light, left the way she wanted to go, gripping the pistol. She swept the beam of her laser sight across the corridor again. At least two. Maybe more. The ones behind her probably came from the unmarked offshoots. The ones in front might have come from those and just wandered up toward Vintooth or there was another unmarked tunnel or two up ahead.

"Surface," said a voice behind her. She turned her head toward it. One of the newcomers had breached the circle of light. Completely naked, he watched her with cloudy blue eyes that looked like someone had put translucent mesh over his irises. He shuffled forward, coming closer. Something in his demeanor sent a warning, and she swung her pistol toward him, training the laser sight on his forehead. He stopped, momentarily confused.

"Back," she said, using a tone that conveyed authority and danger.

He cocked his head. "Surface," he whispered and then launched himself at her, and she fired, moving to her left as his body fell heavily to the floor where she'd been, his head a blackened, smoldering mass of gelatinous flesh and bone. Torri swung the light toward her left, just in time to shoot another attacker. The gelpulse caught him in the torso and exploded out his back, spatter raining across the one behind him, who grunted in surprise and retreated.

She turned her light to the right again. The carnage seemed to have attracted a few more. One tried a similar tactic to his predecessor, and she blew a hole through his thigh. Not enough to kill him, but enough to make him scream and writhe on the floor, kicking and flailing. She let him, thinking it might confuse the others. No time to make her way carefully toward Vintooth. She trained the light in front of her. Six, now. They turned away from the beam, leaving a narrow path between them and the left hand wall.

The hairs on the back of Torri's neck broadcast danger, and she whirled, blasting another one behind her. He screamed, tearing at his abdomen as it dissolved, and three of his comrades fell on him, like starving animals. She turned back toward Vintooth. *Fuck.* Ten, now. She shot one on the left and another on the right, using both the pistol and the light to clear a path, and she started running, shining the light in front of her. Another one appeared twenty paces ahead, loping toward her. She shot him, too, and his body lifted a foot off the ground and fell, flopping, to the right though she had to jump over his legs.

At least one was gaining on her from behind. She heard his breath in his throat, could smell it, too, a rank, decayed odor tinged with lunacy and violence. She ran faster, shooting another in front and dodging as he fell. No time to stop and take out a few behind her. That's all she'd get. A few. The rest would bury her by sheer numbers, no matter how many rounds she had. She ran faster, faster than she thought she could, an eerie keening echoing behind her.

Ahead, she saw another offshoot tunnel, and a form emerging from it. She shot him as she passed but was unprepared for the one that threw himself out of the entrance at her from behind the other. He slammed into her, and his weight propelled her into the left-hand wall, knocking her off balance. She tried to retain her footing but couldn't, and he was on her, screeching and grabbing, dragging her to the floor, tearing her pack off. She fired, turning her head away as the gelpulse blew his torso completely off his legs. The force of the shot littered the walls and ceiling with blood and tissue. She kicked his legs off her and fired again and again at the forms clogging the tunnel behind her. *I'm not going without a fight, slagging fucking...* "And fuck you, too, Rila." She filled the corridor with gelpulses, a steady stream of cuss words and Coalition-bashing accompanying her rapid fire.

Still firing, Torri crab-crawled backward, toward Vintooth, trying to maneuver herself into a position where she could stand and run again. No time. She shot three more, and their bodies momentarily slowed the horde. Using the heartbeat of time she'd bought, she stumbled to her feet and took off running, adrenaline lending her what felt like superhuman speed. Not enough. She went down again, another on her back, his hands around her neck like steel cords. She tried to flip over so she could at least go out shooting but she couldn't find leverage. *So this is it, then. Fucking—*

The man on her back exploded. And the one next to her did, as well. Myriad blue gelpulses hissed above her, thumping into flesh, forcing screams and howls. The smell of singed hair and meat filled the corridor, along with the scuffling of feet on stone as the horde retreated. Torri pressed her forehead to the floor and protected her head with her arms, opting not to draw fire. It seemed to go on for hours, though it was probably only a matter of seconds.

Someone leaned down, and Torri felt a touch on her back. "Stay down."

*Kai.* Torri half-laughed, almost sobbed.

"Grenade," Kai said, and she moved away for a moment.

Torri heard Kai grunt as she made the throw, and then she was lying on Torri's back, another layer of protection as a hollow *whumpf* erupted from somewhere behind them. The initial shockwave rolled over their bodies, a turbulent passage of heat and magnetic force that dissipated within seconds, followed by a second, lesser wave. That too dispersed on its way to Vintooth.

Torri didn't try to get up right away as she waited for her senses to clear. Kai's weight and warmth on her back made her feel cocooned, safe, and she just wanted to cry with relief. She bit her lip instead.

"Please tell me you're all right," Kai said near Torri's left ear, breath hot across her skin.

"I am now," she said around the lump in her throat.

Using the floor as leverage, Kai pushed off Torri's back. "Don't move. I want to check you for wounds."

Torri remained where she was, and Kai's fingers were on her back, shoulders, legs.

"Any bites?" Kai asked, her fingers moving Torri's hair off the back of her neck.

"No. Don't think so. Bruises and scrapes, mostly."

"Roll over."

"Thought you'd never ask," Torri muttered.

Kai decreased the power on her porta-light, knelt, and inspected Torri's neck as Torri lay on her back. It was all Torri could do not to sit up and burrow into her arms. Kai slowly tracked the light down Torri's body, examining her.

"What's the prognosis?" Torri joked.

Kai looked at her, hand on Torri's right knee. "A good chance you're fine physically. Mentally, still insane. Completely." She smiled, relief evident on her features.

Torri sat up. "You're sure? Completely?"

Kai nodded. "Afraid so." She stood and offered her hand.

Torri took it, and Kai hauled her to her feet. She moved around a little, making sure she had no broken bones. "Thank Cyllea. I thought I'd lost my touch and gone only half-insane."

"Oh, no. No halfway at all. Completely. But I always liked that about you," Kai said softly as she pulled Torri into a hug. And Torri held on like it was the last time she'd have the chance, burying her face against Kai's neck, arms wrapped so tightly around her that had Kai tried to extricate herself, it would have been futile.

"Damn you," Torri whispered, before she kissed Kai's skin above her collar. *Collar*. Kai was in uniform. She was in uniform and a half-mile underground, consorting with a "party of interest" as a representative of the Coalition. Kai kissed her before she had a chance to really think about that, and Torri melted into her, as she always did when Kai's lips were on hers. *Damn her*.

"So how is it that you managed to join me on this lovely outing?" Torri murmured against Kai's lips. "While dressed for other occasions?"

Kai brushed Torri's hair out of her face. "You're getting careless in your old age," she teased. "I tracked you through the microcomm I put in your pocket."

Torri started to say something but Kai cut her off.

"Two reasons. I wanted you to find it later but I also had a bad feeling. I hoped nothing would go wrong and you'd leave Newburg without any untoward incidents, but . . ." She shrugged.

"That doesn't really explain how you came to be here. And what kind of signal could you pick up down here?"

"I did lose it. And I knew at that point that something had gone wrong. Lucky for you that part of my responsibilities involves monitoring security reports. Luckier still that a certain Lieutenant Bris Fandiz is a stickler for filing them as soon as she can."

Torri smiled then. "I knew I liked her. So she dropped me off with Major Rila and went to file a report."

Kai reluctantly released her hold. "She did. It helps, too, that I have special dispensation under the increased security directive to be down here. High rank and proven skills have their privileges. But it wouldn't matter whether I did or not. I'd be here anyway." She picked Torri's pistol and porta-light up and handed them to her, making a "tsking" noise as she did so. "You're better with the bigger guns."

Torri re-holstered the blaster. "I see you're packing double." She raised an eyebrow at the holsters on both of Kai's thighs.

Kai started walking, training her porta-light in front of her. "Honey, do you think these guns clash with my uniform?" she asked over her shoulder, deadpan.

*Cyllea, no.* And Torri buried an excruciatingly arousing image of Kai wearing nothing *but* her holsters and pistols. She matched her pace with Kai's. "Might I ask about what just happened?"

Kai was quiet for a moment before responding. "Lost souls, is what the locals call them."

"How did they get here?"

"Don't know. Some were miners who got stuck in brainjacks. I heard that others ended up here after the Collapse, hiding, and never got out. I suspect some of them slagged off local officials." Kai glanced at her. "Or ended up in the middle of a political shitstorm."

"Not something I sought to do," Torri said stiffly, keeping her eyes on the corridor floor in front of her.

Kai gripped Torri's arm, and they both stopped. "You're right about the market squeeze. That's why they've cracked down on Vintooth. There're also local officials here who seem to be interested in taking advantage of it."

Torri refrained from making a sarcastic comment about Major Rila.

"I don't know for certain all the parties involved, and most likely, trying to find out will only put me in a Coalition firefight and get me shipped to some place a lot less pleasant than this. I have some ideas, but the only reason I care is to keep out of it."

"A wise choice," Torri said dryly, studying Kai's face in the light their portables afforded, sensing a shift in her loyalties, in the way her world ordered itself. Or maybe she was simply accepting that realities weren't necessarily beholden to duties.

"And to keep you out of it, too," Kai added.

"Because I'm incapable of doing it myself?" Torri tried not to harden her tone, but from Kai's expression, she was unsuccessful.

Kai sighed, exasperated. "You can't always choose your deals. Cyr talked his way to Rila. There's no way you could have known that. She put the surveillance order on you, though she wasn't the only one who authorized my orders. The only reason I figured Rila might be interested in more than just routine surveillance was through Fandiz's report. She detailed not only escorting you to the interrogation room, but also to Rila. The head of security simply doesn't waste time on a mere surveillance detail unless there's some kind of clear threat."

Torri stopped walking. "That puts Fandiz in an awkward position. Does her family have pull to mitigate anything Rila might do if she finds out her name is in an official Coalition report linked to mine?"

Kai studied her for a while.

"The lieutenant is earnest, serious, and wants to do her duty to the best of her abilities," Torri said at Kai's expression. "But she's naïve and untested. Not material for her position. Somebody must have owed her family a favor and Fandiz was the recipient of the promotion. Either that or the Coalition wanted to show its appreciation for loyalty. And ensure they kept it."

"You should've been an Academy instructor. Psychological profiling."

Torri half-laughed. "And miss out on all the fun down here?" She continued walking, Kai at her side. "How much does Rila know?"

"Enough that you're down here. She knows you're contracted to lift a shipment of pure-colors from Vintooth. Cyr told the informant—your miner—so she figures, what's one more? And if you're not successful, she loses nothing. Gains nothing, either, but nothing can be traced to her. With the possible exception of a few questions that Fandiz's report raises." Kai glanced over at her. "Rila can just say that it was a routine interrogation and she released you back to your ship. Rila, after all, is head of overall security. Most likely, she's already altered Fandiz's report." She sighed. "Fandiz's inexperience will actually protect her and Rila knows that. And as far as you're concerened, you're just an opportunity for her."

Torri nodded. So she'd been right. Rila *was* on the take. And she'd put Torri into a position that turned her either into a Coalition bootlicker or prey for a feral mob of miners. The thought mixed with bile in her throat. She swallowed. "Who's doing the squeeze?"

Kai shook her head. "Don't know. I have a feeling it's not an official here, though. Whoever it is has connections in Newburg and probably higher up."

Torri turned away and glared into the darkness beyond the beams of their lights. *This is a political shitstorm.* "I'm contracted for one shipment," she said, enunciating each word, not caring what Kai thought about her business choices. "But if I don't score two, I won't have any currency left in Newburg. Rila will make sure of that. And if I *do* lift a second shipment for her, she has something on me." Kai said nothing, and Torri pursed her lips, thinking. "An unenviable position." *But one that might, in spite of itself, present options.* "Where are *you* in this?" She focused on Kai again.

"Making sure you get out of Newburg intact."

"That's not what I asked."

Kai ran her free hand through her hair. "I hadn't thought past that."

"There's a whole lot between now and then," Torri said, not unkindly.

"I know." Kai hesitated, and her next words came out in a rush. "But when I lost the signal on the microcomm, I started looking through security reports and found out you'd been taken to Rila. I picked up one ping from the microcomm, and I pinpointed it at a force shield off a main transport tube." She cleared her throat and directed her gaze straight ahead. "It took some work, going through mining maps until I found one that showed an older access tunnel into Vintooth. The only one besides the current main entrance that could get someone into that matrix." She gestured at the wall. "This corridor is on the maps, but it's marked as a cave-in risk and that's pretty much what the official line is, and—I'm rambling." She stopped and took a deep breath, hands on her hips. "Does it really matter how I got here?"

Torri opened her mouth to assure her that it didn't, but Kai interrupted.

"I can't lose you," she blurted.

Delightful little sparks raced through Torri's gut.

"I know what it feels like, to think you're gone." She looked down at the floor then back at Torri. "Hallifin changed things. I never thought I'd see you again. I knew you were alive, but it wasn't necessarily something I thought about. I'm good at compartmentalizing." A little smile flickered at the corners of her mouth. "And then there you were. And I didn't know how to deal with that."

"You seemed to do fine," Torri said, droll.

Kai ignored the comment. "I didn't know how to deal with much of anything, but seeing you—" She cleared her throat. "If I never saw you again after that, I at least had Hallifin. But now here you are in Newburg."

Something worked its way into Torri's bones, settled like a warm blanket across her neurons. "And here you are, as well. So tell me, Captain Tinsdale, about risks."

"What do you mean?"

"'Risk is a balance between what is known and what is not,'" Torri quoted, crossing her arms.

"'What you know comes with experience. And experience comes with risk.'" Kai hooked her thumbs on her belt. "'When weighing a course of action, never risk what you're not willing to lose.'" She grimaced a little. "Instructor Stran made it all seem so academic. Until we flew that third training mission together. Remember that? Turkland Province."

Torri nodded, gratified that Kai had followed her thoughts, had gone immediately to the specific place in their shared past that she herself was picturing. "You took a risk, choosing Valkyrie Canyon over Dark. Everybody else chose Dark and had to abort because of the landslide that blocked Raven's Mouth."

Kai shrugged. "The topo read-outs looked different than the night before. It wasn't a damn sunshadow. The contours weren't right."

"But it was still a risk, because Valkyrie was an expert run, and we hadn't done it together at that point. We hadn't even done it separately."

Kai shrugged again, in the way she did to indicate that something seemed completely obvious to her. "I already knew that we worked well together. And when I made the decision, you looked at the read-outs and then asked if I was sure. You didn't question it when I said I was."

"Because I knew how good a pilot you were then and how

good you'd be later. If you thought the contours weren't right, it was because they weren't right."

Kai smiled conspiratorially. "And that ride was completely worth getting called to Yeldar's office. He was furious, but we were the only ones who completed the course." She nodded, more to herself than Torri. "He flew out the next day and when he saw the landslide in Dark, he shut up about it."

Torri lowered her hands to her sides. "I left the flying to you because even then you were a better pilot than I could ever be. But in matters like this, I think I'm the better pilot."

Kai's eyes narrowed.

"Trust me," Torri said, a plan forming.

"What exactly is the risk?" A note of wary skepticism colored the question.

"Me."

Kai frowned. "No." She turned and started walking again toward Vintooth.

Torri exhaled, preparing to deal with Kai's familiar stubbornness. She caught up with her. "It's the only real option there is."

Kai halted suddenly, whirled. "No." More vehement this time. She resumed walking at a brisk pace.

"Listen to me."

Kai stopped and turned on her, expression in her eyes as hard and uncompromising as unmined opals. "No. Absolutely not. I did not come down here to fucking lose you to another one of your plans." She started walking again.

Torri followed her, swallowing retorts and trying to frame her response better. "Do you honestly think I'd take any kind of chance with the Coalition if I thought they had a good shot at me?"

Kai glared at her.

"Never mind. Don't answer that. How about this? If I thought this wouldn't work, I wouldn't even pose it. You know that. You know if I thought something was completely untenable, I wouldn't even bring it up."

That got her. Kai stopped, training the beam of her porta-light at the floor. "Fair enough."

Torri faced her, and for a moment they were Cadets again, and Torri was trying to convince Kai to sneak out after curfew and go exploring. But there were years and beliefs between them now, no matter the little concessions Kai was making, and the flashes of their old comradeship in her smile. "The only thing that makes sense to do is to get me into Vintooth. I'll make the contact, which will most likely be someone in the workshops. That'll be the shipment Rila wants. No doubt she's got somebody else waiting for it, as well." Something occurred to Torri. "And she'll probably confiscate it legally and pin me with the theft."

"And your solution to this?"

Torri raised an eyebrow. "I'll get Rila's shipment but you, Captain Tinsdale, will do such a good job discovering this heist that you'll foil the attempt."

"But—"

"*After* I pass the shipment to Rila's contact."

Kai tugged thoughtfully on her lower lip for a few moments, comprehension spreading across her features. "The second shipment will be out of your hands. You know the contact?"

"No, but Rila's thorough and the wrist reader she supplied is probably pinging even now."

"What about the other shipment? You need two. One for Rila, one to fulfill your contract." She stated it as if she were talking about a legitimate business deal, much to Torri's surprise.

"My crew has their orders," she said, and she knew Kai wouldn't want specifics.

Kai pursed her lips, still pondering. "Can they pull this off?"

"We'll see."

"That's not what I wanted to hear," Kai half-chided.

Torri shrugged. "'In the absence of static circumstances,'" she quoted, "'every contingency must be considered.' I'm not so untested that I can't be realistic about what could happen. But I'm also not so untested that I overestimate my capabilities."

Kai regarded her, and Torri thought back to that third training mission, when Kai pointed at Valkyrie Canyon on the navscreen and said that was the best way, the only way, given the situation. The roles had been reversed then, but in Kai's expression Torri saw echoes of the inexperienced but gifted pilot and knew that the risk Kai posed in the cockpit of their class two fighter that day so many years ago was within the arena of possibility and that Kai wouldn't suggest it if she didn't have confidence in their ability to adjust and execute successfully.

Kai sighed, and Torri knew she'd relented. On impulse, she ran her fingers along Kai's jaw, surprising even herself with the gesture, and its tenderness.

"Are you sure?" Kai made no effort to move away.

"It's the best way. The only way, given the situation." She cupped Kai's cheek. "Will you trust me?"

Kai leaned into her touch, and a smile reminiscent of the first one she ever offered Torri softened her features. "I always have."

Torri's heart bounced around in her chest like a ship entering an atmosphere at the inflection Kai used. She quelled her feelings, refocused. "Check in with your contingent. Tell them you've found a party of interest near Vintooth and you're bringing her in for questioning."

Kai held her gaze a bit longer, as if she was going to argue another point, but she stepped away and activated her commlink. While she spoke brusquely to whomever she'd contacted, Torri shone her light behind them, sweeping the corridor from side to side. Nothing. No movement. Kai had been thorough. But most likely, they had only a temporary reprieve. She opened her commlink and pinged Saryl again.

"Done," Kai announced.

Torri checked her wrist reader. A half-mile to Vintooth. She held her wrists up. "Cuff me."

Kai hesitated, brow furrowed.

"Do it." She quirked an eyebrow. "And maybe some day I'll let you do it in other circumstances."

Kai rolled her eyes and took a pair of cuffs out of her cargo pocket. She placed them on Torri's wrists and activated them. Their translucent flexi-gel bands glowed pale green in the dim light of the tunnel. "I think I rather like this look on you," she muttered, flashing a wry smile. She took Torri's holster and clipped it onto her own belt. Torri retained the porta-light, holding it in both hands. Kai motioned for her to precede her. "You lead."

"How gracious." Torri held her hands up near her chest and pointed the light down the corridor toward Vintooth. "Shall we?"

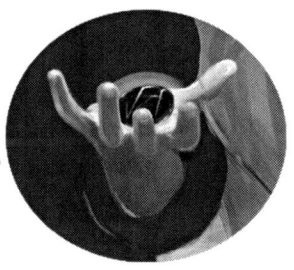

## CHAPTER 12

The closer they got to the main cavern, the more Torri's feet tingled, even through her boot soles. Like at Newburg, the pounding and constant vibration from mining equipment changed the very air in the corridor, which hung like pungent clouds in the increasing heat. Torri pinged Saryl every ten minutes, hoping at least one got through so she could get a read on Torri's general location. A little over an hour to eighteen hundred, though if the crew left without her, it wouldn't necessarily be the end of the world. She'd just have to come up with a plan and meet them elsewhere. Provided she could pull this off. And provided they could, as well. If not . . . she opted not to think about that just yet.

Torri glanced at Kai for the thousandth time. The line of her jaw had hardened, and Kai was completely in uniform again, though Torri knew what she kept hidden underneath, knew that the Coalition slid off her skin like any pair of trousers. Had she been questioning in Hallifin? Perhaps, and only using the excuse that when she was in uniform, things might be different between them. Watching her now, Torri doubted that. Something had changed between them, supplanting the uniform with their past, and Kai no longer seemed to fight that, as she had since they'd graduated, since she'd been on the other side of the chasm.

And now what? A bridge, maybe. A connection Kai was no longer denying, no longer avoiding. And actively cultivating.

Torri shifted her attention to the corridor, hearing not only machinery but the faint hum of a barrier, and indeed, a few seconds later they arrived at a force shield, and Torri surmised this corridor had been the "back way" Saryl had found, the one allegedly unused because of a cave-in. Kai commed someone, and a few seconds later the barrier flickered and dissolved. Torri went first, another hundred yards into the main tunnel that would take them toward the Vintooth entrance.

Kai grasped Torri's left arm, giving it a quick, comforting squeeze as they entered the busy main tunnel. Here, mining personnel and equipment filled the corridor, involved in the business at hand, talking to each other or moving purposefully to their next tasks. A few glanced at them, but Kai's uniform probably made them direct their attention elsewhere as quickly as they could.

The noise and heat were almost unbearable here, and Torri gritted her teeth, fighting an urge to bolt for the entrance. Kai guided her through the crowd, and no matter how it looked, a Coalition captain and a party of interest, Torri was immensely glad for her presence. She concentrated for a moment and sent another ping to Saryl. Had they been able to leave the docks? Would Rila have granted them departure clearance?

She waited for an overloaded floater bearing miners to pass, its hull nearly scraping the ground. A high-pitched tone rang through her skull, and relief washed through her. Saryl, pinging her back. They had a lock on her. Now it just remained to be seen if they could acquire the shipment of pure-colors that Majan had contracted. Torri had every confidence that Saryl and Jann would come up with a viable plan. And if Saryl felt it wouldn't work, she'd abort the operation and instead find a way to extricate Torri from the bowels of Newburg.

Torri thought briefly of Jindor. She'd have to trust that Saryl would jettison her if she suspected that Jindor might be cloaking. And if not, then they just might have a new navigator.

She sent two answering pings, a signal of acknowledgement, and breathed a sigh of relief.

Kai navigated her into the cavern that housed the workshop. Though the Coalition Directives had severely curtailed shipping, mining hadn't stopped. So what was the Coalition going to do with all those opals? Maybe glut a different quadrant and squeeze a few others. That made sense. Torri guessed Endor was experiencing a squeeze, since that's where Majan's client requested they make the delivery. Some Coalition official wanting to make extra money, most likely. At three hundred thousand or more for each stone, a hundred opals could go a long way.

And a relatively easy way to do it, especially if the official had pull, which Torri suspected was the case. No way to directly link the Alpha Quadrant problems with Endor through the client, after all. Besides, markets fluctuated all the time. Whoever the client was, he was going to make a fortune in a very short period of time.

Torri kept a step ahead of Kai, so it appeared that Kai was bringing her in for interrogation. They approached a door near the workshop, and the Coalition guard nearest the keypad opened it when he saw Kai. He and the other three saluted, and Kai acknowledged the gesture with a brusque nod. They entered a room not unlike the one in which Torri had met Rila. A quick survey indicated that Kai was the ranking officer on duty, and that plus the way Kai comported herself brought the ten other soldiers in the room to immediate attention. No sloppiness here. Kai wouldn't tolerate it.

"Captain," said the ranking lieutenant, her gaze straight ahead.

"Report," Kai responded.

"Security detail has completed two sweeps of the workshops. Nothing required attention."

"Excellent." Kai glanced at Torri then back at the lieutenant. "That might change."

The lieutenant looked at Torri then, and Kai unfastened Torri's cuffs. "This is Trader Syl t'Dorrin, who had the vast misfortune of contracting with the wrong parties on this particular trip to Newburg." Kai placed herself directly in front of Torri, staring into her eyes, allowing perhaps a foot of space between them. Probably a technique she used during interrogations. Intimidating, in other circumstances. Torri pretended wariness.

"Fortunately," Kai pronounced with typical Coalition gravity, "Trader t'Dorrin realized what had happened—though almost too late—and has agreed to cooperate fully with us in bringing some dishonest marketing to an end."

Torri lowered her gaze first, knowing Kai's underlings would note the gesture. "I am at your service, Captain. My apologies for my error. Had I known the nature of my former client, I most certainly would not have allowed things to progress to this point." She shrugged helplessly. "Though I have been conducting business for several years and I screen my contracts copiously, a less-than-legitimate party occasionally slips through."

Kai nodded sagely. "The nature of all business. But a situation remedied through your quick thinking, Trader." Kai turned then and addressed the soldiers. "Trader t'Dorrin is privy to information in which someone will attempt to steal a shipment from the workshops. This party is most likely someone employed in the workshops. Trader t'Dorrin has informed me that the party is able to track her, much to her chagrin. Though the trader has discovered the source of the link and apprised me of it." Kai walked down the line of guards. "She has also agreed to act as bait so that we might determine who this thief is and whether he or she has other contacts in the workshops. Chances are, it's someone acting in tangent with someone based in the city, but in this line of work—" Kai stopped, waiting.

"We examine every angle, Captain," said the guards in unison.

"And?"

"We use every tool at our disposal, Captain."

Kai nodded in such a way that for a moment she reminded Torri of Flight Instructor Milor, who had been a favorite among Cadets. No-nonsense and not one to be crossed, but eminently fair. He inspired even the most inept to work as hard as possible to win his approval. Like Milor's, Kai's respect was hard-earned but once it was, it inspired those who served with her to strive to keep it. Torri had seen flashes of Kai's leadership abilities at the Academy, but here, in the Vintooth matrix guardroom, she saw yet another reason that Kai was so good at what she did.

"Excellent. Lieutenant, you and Privates Northi and Drex will conduct surveillance with me. Corporal Tredin, choose three and take the perimeter. Do not engage with Trader t'Dorrin unless under my order. As far as you're concerned, you have no idea who she is. Observation only until she makes contact. Clear?"

"Clear," came the response in unison.

"Five minutes. Tredin's team first. Northi and Drex, on my order."

They all saluted on one accord, and within twenty seconds Tredin had assembled his crew and assigned them positions. Cogs in a well-ordered and highly efficient machine. Kai's hand at work, Torri knew. Not for the first time, she wondered if maybe they would have had a better chance at Shanlin if Kai had joined the Resistance rather than shipping out for officer training in Vector Quadrant. Typical of the Coalition. Divide and conquer, attack from many fronts. Behind the scenes, the power brokers bought loyalty or ensured it through well-placed assassinations. They'd been maneuvering for years. Probably since Torri and Kai were children.

"Trader t'Dorrin? Are you ready?"

Torri looked at Kai. "Ready, Captain."

Kai nodded toward the entrance. "Let's see what we find."

Torri exited first. She didn't know how long Kai would wait before following, but she knew onlookers would not be able to discern a connection between her or Kai's team. For that she was grateful, since Rila's contact might be watching, as well as tracking. Torri worked her way through the crush of miners and light equipment until she arrived at the Vintooth workshops. She lingered outside, waiting for Rila's contact to show himself. Or herself.

Torri leaned against the wall and scanned the crowd. A couple of others were engaged in similar behavior outside the workshops, so her actions probably wouldn't attract attention. She wasn't sure where Kai or her teams were, but she knew Kai was observing everything, along with the soldiers she'd inducted into this venture, under the pretense that Torri was bait, a hapless and unfortunate trader who got into something a little too deep. She suspected this was how Kai broke so many smuggling rings. She found the weak link and followed it right up the chain.

But this time, the weak link was on the other end of the wrist reader in Torri's pocket, the one Rila had supplied. Torri had turned it on fifteen minutes ago, and it picked up a ping from the workshops. So Rila's contact was perfectly positioned to supply a shipment of pure-colors. All Rila needed was someone to take the fall, and either end of the chain remained intact. A good plan. Smart. But not foolproof.

"Excuse me," a reedy, raspy voice said in Coalition.

Torri looked to her left at the owner of the voice. She lowered her gaze, as the speaker stood no more than four feet tall. She wore a silver apron that hugged her body but the only way Torri knew she was female was because of the Frin's size. Males almost always stood Torri's height or taller. Females almost never broke five feet.

"Your order is ready," the Frin said, her facial scales slowly pulsing blue.

"Thank you." Torri nodded once, as if she had, in fact, been waiting for some kind of order. She followed the Frin into the workshop, where several carvers were at work at tables behind a sleek black counter that came up to Torri's waist and stretched fifty feet across. Each carver had an individual station, well-lit, and the soft whine of stonecutting tools mixed with the dull roar of the drill rigs from the depths of the matrix.

The Frin gestured at the counter. "Wait, please." She went around the counter into the work area, and Torri looked up at the cavern roof, some twenty feet above. Sentry pods hovered between the ceiling and the floor, some ten feet above. Five other customers stood on her side of the counter. Two robed Miridians with one human, and a dark-skinned human with a Talesian. Torri turned her attention back to the work tables. Vintooth had some of the finest carvers in Austra Province. One slip of the tool, even a micron, and a pure-color black could be ruined. A good carver might produce one standard cut every two days. The more unusual cuts might require six, though she'd heard about a Vintooth carver who'd done a star cut in three days.

"Your order," said the Frin, placing a silver shipment case on the counter. She stood Torri's height now, and Torri guessed that a ramp ran the length of the counter on the opposite side.

Torri gripped the handle with her left hand. "Many thanks."

The Frin's face betrayed nothing and her scales continued to pulse blue. Nothing untoward, then. But what now? She left the workshop carrying the case. Kai could question the Frin, but chances were she knew nothing except to fill an order. She was too low on the ladder. So the most obvious thing to do was to start toward the entrance. There had to be another contact. Maybe the Frin alerted whomever that was. Kai would wait until the second link in the chain appeared before she moved in.

Torri pinged Saryl as she made her way through the massive cavern that housed the workshops. Saryl had pinged her again a few minutes earlier. She had a read on Torri though what she planned to do with that Torri didn't know. Through the crowd, Torri thought she caught a glimpse of Kai's uniform. She pushed through a group of miners standing around a vending station when someone jostled her from behind.

"Let go of the case," said a gruff male voice in Empire. The inflection he used carried a threat.

Torri sidestepped, stalling, and pretended to get in line at the vending station. She set the case on the floor, next to her right foot. He fell in line behind her. Torri felt rather than saw him pick up the container and leave the line.

"Hey!" she shouted after him. "Thief!"

He stopped and turned, confusion on his broad, bland features. Torri recognized him then. The Earthman Cyr had paid at Shintal's. And he hadn't expected her reaction. Torri didn't have time to consider that because he broke into a run, headed for the main entrance. Kai was right behind him, followed closely by two black-clad regular enlisted soldiers. Torri left the line as well, running after Kai. Might as well act like she was trying to do the right thing by the Coalition. The thought chafed her but where Kai was concerned, Torri would do what she could.

She saw Kai's back in the crowd and increased her speed, dodging onlookers and people trying to get out of her way. Just past Kai's shoulder she saw the Earthman's brown shirt. The knots of people parted for him—no great love for the Coalition—and Torri sped up again, trying to flank Kai and maybe head him off before he reached the entrance. No doubt at least one of the officers there was in Rila's pocket.

And then she was stumbling, tripping as the crowd

constricted in the corridor that led outside. The man in front of her also lost his balance, and she fell on top of him. He grunted and swore in Empire. Torri rolled off him and staggered to her feet, slamming into someone else. She spun, nearly tripped again, but a hand on her upper arm steadied her, pulled her close, out of the flow of the crowd.

"Here, now, what's this about?" asked the hand's owner in Coalition.

Torri fought a grin and instead looked up at Saryl. "A thief. He's got a full shipment on him." She ignored the throbbing of her various bruises.

Saryl stared down at her, disapproving. "That's a matter for proper authorities, I'd warrant." Still gripping Torri's arm, she pulled her against the right-hand wall of the corridor, where four black-uniformed soldiers directed pedestrian and floater traffic around something Torri couldn't yet see. She allowed Saryl to drag her through a few onlookers to a grey-uniformed woman standing over a form lying on the corridor's floor.

"Captain," Saryl said, with the proper Coalition fawning, "Another party of interest, perhaps?" She released Torri's arm and stepped back. Kai directed one of the rank-and-files to stand guard over the prone Earthman.

"My thanks for your vigilance, Agent."

Torri appraised Saryl again. She wore the dark blue trousers and shirt of private security.

"Captain, if I may?" Jindor's voice. "I'd like to retrieve my own shipment," she said, pointing at a silver case lying against the right-hand wall. She was dressed in the robes of a merchant and held a second case indistinguishable from the first.

"Of course," Kai assented, and Jindor retrieved the case against the wall and brought the other to Kai. "You're all right?" Kai asked.

"Yes, thank you," Jindor said as she approached Kai. "I managed to get out of his way before he knocked me completely over. Your man there dropped this one," she said in Coalition, handing one of the cases to Kai.

"May I trouble you," Kai said as she took the case, "to accompany me to the workshops that we might straighten this out?"

"Most assuredly," Jindor said, flashing a disarming smile.

Kai issued an order to two other rank-and-files who hauled the Earthman to his feet. One cuffed his hands behind his back. They marched him back through the corridor, the crowds parting easily.

"Trader t'Dorrin, I appreciate your help in this but I'd like you to come with us." Kai maintained smooth professionalism.

Torri nodded once. "Certainly." And she followed Kai back toward the workshops, Saryl and Jindor behind her. Within a few minutes, she stood once again at the counter. The Frin's scales pulsed a little faster and those beneath her cheeks shifted to deep red. Kai pretended not to notice as she overrode the seal on the case Jindor had given her. She waited a moment for the override to take effect, then opened it, laying it flat on the counter and gesturing at the trays therein.

"Are these Vintooth?" she asked the Frin, whose taloned fingers pulsed pink with agitation.

The Frin picked one up and studied it. The red tinge from her scales dissipated. "One moment," she said. She set the stone on the counter and commed someone. A few moments later, a carver approached from his workbench wearing a silver apron like the Frin's.

"Yes?" He wiped his hands on a cloth.

"Appraisal," she said, motioning at the case.

He picked up the stone she'd left on the counter and examined it for a few seconds. "Huh," he said. He took the first tray out of the case and studied it. Then the second. And third. Each of the ten he took out and regarded. He then put all the trays back. "Synthetic. All of them." He shrugged, puzzled but not terribly concerned. "Good fakes, and modeled after Vintooth syns, but the buff marks are Slatelock."

The Frin's scales returned to their normal, calm blue, and she dismissed him with a grunt.

Kai turned to the thief. "Does your contact know you arranged to steal syns?" He said nothing, and Kai beckoned at one of the rank-and-file soldiers. "Your palm reader," she instructed, and he handed it to her. She triggered it with her thumb and studied the screen, moving her thumb around on the pad until she had what she wanted. She showed the reader to the Earthman. He looked at it but maintained silence though his jaw muscles clenched. Kai glanced at Torri. "Trader t'Dorrin, do you know this man?"

Torri approached and looked at the screen. "I do. Rozin Hester, former navigator on my ship."

"Where is he now?"

"I don't know, Captain. I unfortunately had to dismiss him from service. The report is on file with hangar security."

The Earthman blanched. Kai called up another image and showed it to him. He looked at it then moved his gaze to the floor. Kai showed it to Torri. "And this?"

Torri looked at the picture of Major Rila and furrowed her brow. "Seems familiar. I may have seen her at a Coalition security check-point near the city mines." She'd leave responsibility for revealing Rila's role in this to the Earthman. If he did so, Rila couldn't trace that back to Torri, and that meant Rila owed her, if their paths crossed again. *In an unfamiliar game, always keep more than you bet.*

Kai cleared the reader, and the picture of Major Rila faded, to be replaced by an image of the Earthman. "Dinil Folath. Recent transfer to this matrix from the city mines." She pursed her lips. "One other name appears in conjunction with your biometric profile." She entered another code. "Criminal activity under that other name." She handed the reader back to the rank-and-file soldier. "I think perhaps we need to take a little trip back to Newburg." To his guards she said, "I'll accompany. Prepare a floater for transport."

Each guard on either side of Folath saluted. They moved their prisoner to the workshop entrance, where they stood, waiting.

"Merchant?" Kai addressed Jindor.

"Serizia."

"Merchant Serizia. Might I check the contents of your case?"

Jindor smiled and inclined her head. "Yes," she said and handed it to Kai, who set it on the counter next to the other one. Torri flicked a glance at Jindor, who ignored her and stood watching Kai impassively. Saryl stood behind her, arms crossed. Jindor could have leaned her head back against Saryl's forearms.

Kai overrode the code on the case with a standard security clearance, and the seal released. The Frin called the carver over again. He went through, tray by tray, as he had with the other.

"All real. I carved this tray," he said proudly, pointing to number six.

"Purchase record?" Kai addressed Jindor.

"Majan Pure-Colors," Jindor responded, handing a microcomm to Kai, who slid it into her wrist reader. Barely ten seconds passed before she ejected it.

"My thanks." She handed the comm back to Jindor then she looked up at the Frin, who took a palm reader from her pocket. She triggered it, accessed some records, and handed the reader to Kai.

Torri stood watching as Kai studied the reader. She hooked her thumbs on her belt and winced as pain zipped up her right arm. She lowered her hands so that they hung by her sides instead. She'd need a pain-blocker later on, given what she'd been through today. Kai probably would, as well, though she didn't show it.

"Thank you," Kai said, handing the reader back. Torri caught the Frin's eye, but read nothing in the flat amber irises. She was covering her ass, too, and Torri appreciated that. No doubt the Frin served as Rila's lackey on occasion, and the Coalition turned a blind eye to any other activities she might have going on the side. It wasn't *her* fault Rila's other man got found out, after all. The Frin moved to another customer, and Torri looked at Kai, who was addressing Jindor.

"Merchant Serizia, I appreciate your cooperation. Safe journeys to you." She closed the case and slid it over to Jindor, who programmed it with a code and handed it to Saryl.

Kai closed the case of synthetics and sealed it. She picked it up off the counter then. "You will all accompany me to the entrance, so as to avoid delay in another security check with regard to this shipment."

"I'd be most grateful," Jindor said, inclining her head.

Kai turned her attention to Torri. "Trader t'Dorrin, my apologies to you for the unfortunate circumstances that have inconvenienced you. We'll find Hester and see what else he might have been doing."

"My thanks, Captain. It's been a relief dealing with someone of your caliber and professionalism." *And getting you alone and undressed. May I have opportunities to do it again.* Would she? *Cyllea, to get her alone again.* She forced herself to focus on the present.

"Please," Kai entreated, motioning toward the workshop entrance where the two guards stood with Folath. Kai's fingers brushed Torri's back in a gesture that wouldn't attract attention but that conveyed reassurance and recognition of what linked them. Torri carried the warmth of that touch and the feel of Kai's thigh against hers in the floater on the ride to Vintooth's entrance, where evening left half of the matrix's bowl in shadow.

Folath sat in the back, flanked on either side by a soldier.

He hadn't spoken since the workshop, and Torri wondered if he'd implicate Rila. Most likely, she'd hang him out to dry if he tried that so he'd bring Cyr into the mix. She thought about Cyr's service with her and the man he'd been before his addiction realigned his priorities and robbed him of the integrity she knew he'd had once. She felt no sadness about Cyr's impending downfall. Everyone made choices. He'd made the wrong ones.

Kai spoke with the ranking security officer, who waved them past the crowds. The floater's black-uniformed pilot brought the vehicle to a stop. Saryl climbed out and offered her hand to Jindor, who took it as she, too, exited the craft.

"Trader t'Dorrin, our lander is here, and we can take you back to Newburg if you require a ride," Jindor said pleasantly, with no trace of anything beyond solicitousness in her tone. "It's not too far out of our way, and we do have fuel enough."

"I'd appreciate that, Merchant." Torri eased out of the floater, favoring her bruised right knee. Whether she injured it prior to arriving at Vintooth or not, she didn't know. Nor did she care. She just wanted something to numb the pain and alleviate the stiffness in her limbs. And a hot shower. And then bed. And another night with Kai, who helped her out of the vehicle, a flash of concern in her eyes. Torri shook her head almost imperceptibly and held Kai's gaze, letting her know she'd be all right, and the look Kai gave her sent little shockwaves from her heart to her feet. *More than just one more night, Cyllea help me.*

"Should you return to Newburg in the near future, Trader," Kai said in Coalition, "and should you require any sort of assistance, ask at the nearest security post for me."

"My thanks, Captain. And should you ever have need of a trader—" Torri paused. "You have my name." She turned away before she breached decorum and wrapped Kai in an embrace, made all the harder because she saw the same desire in Kai's eyes. Torri had refrained, too, from using the Academy expression of leave-taking, not wanting to reveal more than what already hung in the space between them.

Instead she gritted her teeth and followed Saryl and Jindor toward the landing pad on the other side of the bowl. Saryl carried the case in her left hand, and her tall frame dwarfed Jindor, though Torri detected an easy rapport between them. She threw a glance over her shoulder, and Kai lifted her hand in a barely discernible wave. Torri's eyes stung, but not from the dust in the evening breezes. She quickened her pace until she was between Saryl and Jindor.

"So how was *your* day, honey?" Saryl asked, flashing a grin.

"Slagged. And I'd kiss both of you right now, but I don't want the Coalition getting any kind of improper ideas."

Saryl laughed. "I was telling Jindor that it's never a dull moment working with you."

Torri grimaced and cast a sidelong glance at Jindor. "So. It seems you've successfully weathered the interview process. Feel like casting your lot with the likes of us?"

"Are you saying I've passed your test, Trader?" she shot back with a smile.

"From my perspective, yes. But I'll leave the final decision to Birrit and Dal, since I was a bit indisposed for a large part of today."

Saryl bumped Torri's shoulder.

"Careful," Torri said with a grimace. "There aren't many parts of me that haven't sustained a bruise and that's not one of them."

"Sorry. Dal will have you patched up in no time." She looked past her at Jindor. "You're hired." To Torri, she said, "And I'm looking forward to hearing the tales of your day. We have a few of our own, as well. It's quite unfortunate, too. We seem to be missing a shipment of Vintooth syns." She sighed in mock exasperation.

"Truly tragic," Torri said with a matching sigh. "We'll have to make do with the real thing." She shook her head but smiled and waited as Saryl triggered the lander's hatch. Jindor entered and took the copilot seat. Torri took one in the back and clicked her harness into place. Saryl stowed the case of opals in a cargo hatch and then settled into the pilot's seat, already adjusted for her height. She closed the hatch, and it lowered with a hiss then sealed with a click and a thick, suction sound. Saryl opened a comm to the Far Seek, probably waiting just offworld, if they'd gone according to plan.

"Go ahead," came Jann's voice. Torri exhaled in relief.

"We have the last bit of cargo, and we'll be flying over Newburg and catching a trajectory from there. ETA . . ." She hesitated as Jindor plotted on the navscreen. "Forty-three minutes."

"Forty-three minutes. Out." Jann broke contact, and Saryl engaged the engines and changed the comm frequency.

Torri settled into the seat. Ten minutes to Newburg, tops, then they'd hurtle up to the ship. Exhaustion, stiffness, and pain dragged at her bones.

"Lander FS-1 requesting departure clearance," Saryl said in Coalition as she adjusted the thrusters.

"You are cleared, Lander FS-1," said a male voice in response. No doubt Kai had cleared the bureaucracy for them.

"Lifting off. Out." Saryl guided the craft upward until it crested the lip of the bowl and then employed the thrusters, and they shot toward Newburg in the encroaching nightfall. Below, the lights of floaters bounced off the track between Vintooth and the city, and Torri focused on one, imagining Kai in it, wondering if maybe she looked up as they passed.

Torri stared out the front window of the bridge, the blackness of space resonating with her current state of mind. She'd slept for nearly twelve hours, and the pain-numbing agent Jann had administered did wonders for the physical aches and bruises she'd acquired on this trip. Her emotional state was another matter, however.

Jindor sat to her left, plotting their course through Endor Quadrant for the drop. Maybe sensing Torri's mood, she'd kept conversation to a minimum, something Torri appreciated. Behind her, Saryl and Jann were going over supplies and upcoming maintenance. They, too, had kept their distance.

Her thoughts returned to Kai yet again, where they'd been nonstop since Vintooth. Something had changed between them. Torri knew it, and she knew Kai knew, as well. She rubbed her eyes with the thumb and index finger of one hand. They'd gone deeper this time, and though Torri wouldn't trade the time they'd spent—regardless of circumstances—for anything, she worried what the shift meant. And was either of them ready to explore what it might entail? She hadn't played the microcomm Kai had left in Torri's pocket. It was sitting in a small depression on her desk in her private quarters. She wasn't sure she was ready to hear Kai's voice again.

"Connections can be the best and worst things in the world," Jindor said quietly, eyes on the screen as her fingers flew over the controls.

Torri looked at her, not entirely surprised at Jindor's intuition. Malrusians were better at observation than humans. She swallowed the sarcastic comment that filled her mouth. No sense treating her crew badly just because she was caught up in some kind of . . . something over a woman. "How so?"

"What you know makes you want more." Jindor entered the final coordinates and turned to face Torri. "What you *don't* know holds you back."

Torri stared at her for a long moment before she smiled.

"You're right." She raised her voice so she could address them all. "My apologies. I haven't been my usual charming self this past day."

Jann and Saryl looked at her, and Saryl rolled her eyes.

Torri continued, "I fly with the best crew in any quadrant. I'm proud to serve with you."

"And I with you," Saryl said, grinning with a mixture of humor and relief.

"Same," Jann added.

"So far, I feel at home." The inflection Jindor used expressed newfound loyalties.

Torri squeezed her shoulder. "So let's make this damn drop and maybe take a week for other things."

"I don't know . . . I was hoping we could fly right up the High Council's ass and steal the wrist reader off each one," Jann said plaintively.

Saryl nodded thoughtfully. "Speaking of—" she started. She unfolded herself from her chair and in two strides stood at Torri's right side. "Thought you'd be interested in these." She dug four pure-color black opals out of one of her pockets. Torri cupped her hands, and Saryl placed them within, their surfaces clicking together.

Torri placed them in her lap and held each up, examining them. "Real." She raised an eyebrow and looked up at Saryl.

"We didn't tell you this part. After you got dumped under Newburg, Jann got a read on Cyr. About the same time, we received clearance to leave. Rila might have been hoping to get rid of all of us at once. At any rate, we had an hour so Jann found Cyr and—" She shrugged. "Payment for the shit he'd started."

"Cyr had these on him?" Torri glanced at Jann, who nodded.

"Plus some fire opals, but I let him keep those, out of the goodness of my heart," he said.

Torri grinned. "Never let it be said that you're not a kind and giving soul. What are you going to do with them?"

"One each." He returned her grin. "We're a family. Sort of."

Torri tossed one to him, and he caught it. She handed another to Saryl. Jindor refused.

"I haven't earned it," she said, shaking her head.

Jann snorted. "Neither did we. An opportunity presented itself, and I availed myself of it. One's yours. Think of it as your first paydisk. We tend to share quite a bit on this vessel." He waggled his eyebrows.

Jindor looked first at the opal Torri held out to her then at Torri's face. "You're sure?"

"It's Jann's decision. You heard him. Besides, you earned it, on this last venture."

Jindor took the stone. "My thanks, Jann."

"So what's after the drop?" Saryl leaned against the bulkhead. "Any new clients?"

"I did get a comm from one of Bultor's network over in Vector. Easy job, good money." Torri held the opal in her palm and stroked its surface with her thumb.

"Define 'easy,' " Saryl teased.

"Jackprobes on an interplanetary run, all in Vector. Think you can handle that?"

"I don't know." Saryl stroked her chin thoughtfully. "You know how I'd prefer to dress up and walk right into a Coalition Council meeting."

"Later. How is everyone for another trip to Earth after the jackprobe run?" Torri glanced around the bridge.

"Another Newburg shipment?" Jann ran a hand over his scalp. "You sure that's wise?"

"No. Amer Province, southwestern region."

Saryl looked at her, puzzled.

"I have a contact who greatly appreciates spices from the

same region we're making the opal drop. If we bring him a supply, he'll pay triple."

"And?" Saryl pressed.

Torri studied the stone in her palm and glanced up at her. "I need to find out which Coalition officials are responsible for the Vegas sector, and which are creating the military base out of the Tinsdale holdings."

"This isn't about a contract is it?" Saryl softened her tone.

Torri held the stone up, and its interior flashed green, blue, and red fire as the lights from the control panel reflected off it. "No, not really. It's more about wanting to repay a favor."

"I don't care what it's about," Jann said. "If it involves fucking the Coalition, I'm in."

Saryl started laughing. "As am I."

Torri turned toward Jindor. "Whatever decision you make, we won't think less of you."

A little smile played at the corners of Jindor's mouth. "I knew I'd like this job. I'm in, too."

Torri sat back, pleased. "Have we any Ryzin Solstice? I think a toast is in order."

"Coming up." Jann left the bridge, Saryl behind him. The stone had warmed in Torri's hand, and she continued to stroke its surface, thinking about the way Kai smiled, and how her eyes said more than her lips ever could, though her lips had their own language.

"Is it about connections?" Jindor asked after a while, a quizzical expression on her face.

Torri closed her fingers over the opal. "Maybe." She stared out the window again, at the pinpoints of stars, and they made her think of the lights of floaters in the darkness beneath a lander, following a track bound for Newburg. She stood and slid the stone into her pocket.

# About the Author

Andi Marquette was born in New Mexico, grew up in Colorado, then ended up back in New Mexico where she completed a Ph.D. in history after two other degrees in anthropology. Around 1993, she became a professional editor and has been obsessed with words ever since, which may or may not be a good thing. She wandered east and spent three years on the other side of the Mississippi, but couldn't shake the West off her boots or out of her soul, so she returned to her homelands and is currently based in Colorado where she edits, writes, and spends lots of time running around in the surrounding mountains.

Her website is at http://andimarquette.com/

# Other Books From Mindancer Press

Adijan and Her Genie
L-J Baker

Tales of Emoria
The Saga of Jame and Tigh
Book 1: Future Dreams
Book 2: Present Paths
by T.J. Mindancer

Emoria Campfire Tales
New Tales of Emoria, Book 1
by T.J. Mindancer

Into the Yellow and Other Stories
by Barbara Davies

available from

Mindancer Press
a division of
Bedazzled Ink Publishing Company
http://www.bedazzledink.com/mindancer

Printed in the United States
147690LV00012B/80/P